THREE-DECKER
MURDER
IN A
NUTSHELL

THREE-DECKER MURDER
IN A
NUTSHELL

A Nutshell Murder Mystery

Frances McNamara

First published by Level Best Books/Historia 2024

This novel is entirely a work of fiction. The names, characters and incidents portrayed in it are the work of the author's imagination. Any resemblance to actual persons, living or dead, events or localities is entirely coincidental.

Frances McNamara asserts the moral right to be identified as the author of this work.

First edition

ISBN: 978-1-68512-475-5

This book was professionally typeset on Reedsy.
Find out more at reedsy.com

For my grandparents who lived in East Boston at the time of this story. Mr. and Mrs. William H. Ellis, Jr. and Mr. and Mrs. Michael J. McNamara

Praise for Frances McNamara's Previous Novels

"Once again, Frances McNamara brings together the "dynamic duo" of Frances Glessner Lee and Dr. George Magrath, who use the evolving field of forensic science to lead the reader through their methodical journey of investigation. Magrath's decades of experience and Lee's inquisitive mind that "work(ed) with the accurate precision of a railroad watch," according to Perry Mason novelist Erle Stanley Gardner, chart a course that keeps the reader on the edge of their seat, until the clues sprinkled throughout the story come together for an exciting conclusion."—William Tyre, Executive Director and Curator Glessner House

"*Three-Decker Murder in a Nutshell* plunges the reader into early police forensics, class divisions, and immigrant rivalries, all couched in 1919 Boston's issues and its historical personalities. Fanny Lee again works with coroner Jake Magrath in this intriguing tale of murder to puzzle through facts and assumptions in a time of social and economic turmoil." —Edith Maxwell, Agatha Award-winning author of the Quaker Midwife Mysteries

"As a writer of contemporary police procedurals, I was fascinated by the lore of an earlier time. By the depiction of emerging forensic science, the nutshell models that helped to solve crimes, and by the very real class prejudices in the Boston of that time. A great read."—Kate Flora, award-winning author of the Joe Burgess series.

Praise for Molasses Murder in a Nutshell

"Overall, *Molasses* is a real treat. Settings and back stories about the time period run smoothly. Particularly delicious is the unexpected denouement. This reader, for one, looks forward to the next Nutshell mystery."—*Historical Novel Society*

"What a wonderful little book!! A mix of historical characters and situations with a clever murder mystery and you've got a great story. Tightly wound, but a little murky in the middle. Great ending, keeps you on the edge of your seat until the end. Highly recommended."—Brazos Booksellers

Comments from other GoodReads and Amazon reviewers

- "I really enjoyed this cozy mystery with a female lead. I also loved the connection to 'nutshells'. I always enjoy reading about women who 'step out of their comfort zones along with societal expectations…'"
- "A well written, fast paced historical mystery. Great fun to read. Will definitely keep an eye out for further books in this series!"
- "A good start for a new historical fiction mystery series. I'll be looking for Book 2."
- "A good historical mystery, based on a fascinating idea, and compelling. The mystery is solid, the characters well developed and the I liked the storytelling."
- "*Molasses Murder in a Nutshell* is highly recommended for history nerds who are a fan of murder mysteries."

Praise for the Emily Cabot Mysteries

"Historical mystery readers who enjoy female sleuths and action firmly centered in realistic portraits of the past will find *Death in a Time of Spanish Flu* a compelling story… Libraries looking for powerful blends of history and mystery which present a sense of place that feels familiar and is engrossing to modern readers (even those who normally don't read books from either genre) will relish the realistic and personal portrait that makes *Death in a*

Time of Spanish Flu hard to put down."—*Midwest Book Review*

"Set in 1918 Chicago, McNamara's excellent ninth Emily Cabot mystery (after 2020's *Death on the Home Front*) finds Emily's physician husband, Stephen, serving on the front lines of the Spanish Influenza epidemic... The real-life characters mingle seamlessly with the fictional ones to capture the myriad contradictions of Chicago, from the dirty politicians and gangsters who run the city to the idealists, intellectuals, and revolutionaries who are committed to social change. This timely novel informs as much as it entertains."—*Publisher's Weekly*

"McNamara's suspenseful third Emily Cabot mystery...convincingly recreates a pivotal moment in American labor history...Laurie King and Rhys Bowen fans will be delighted."—*Publishers Weekly*

"McNamara...proves, if anyone was asking, that librarians make great historical mystery writers... I'd follow Emily to any location."—*Historical Novels Review*

Chapter One

Boston Harbor, Dec. 1, 1919

You assumed it was an accident? You *assumed* she fell? Didn't you even examine the body?" Jake stopped in front of the detective, hunching over to fight off the cold breeze.

Frances Glessner Lee snuggled into her fur coat, peering out from under her astrakhan hat. A chill wind knifed through any uncovered spot as the ferry chugged away from Boston's North End. She was determined to stay on deck for the short ride to East Boston. She sheltered behind the bridge house while medical examiner Dr. George "Jake" Magrath frowned at an embarrassed young police detective.

As she watched her friend Jake tramp back and forth, she thought perhaps she should follow his example. The constant movement probably kept him warm. A flaming anger propelled him. He scolded the young detective as he tromped by.

Detective Peter Attwood was very young. He froze under Jake's accusing stare. The tall and lanky detective's head was encased in a red knit hat that matched a bulky pair of mittens. He looked about twelve years old to forty-one-year-old Fanny, but she knew he must be at least twenty.

Attwood pushed down the red and yellow scarf wrapped around his neck to answer. "We were told she had fallen from the third-floor porch. So, we took her away as quickly as possible. It seemed indecent to leave the poor woman lying face down in the dirt." Attwood's nose and cheeks were scorched red either by the wind or embarrassment.

Jake looked up. Both of the men squinted against the wind. "And it was only when the funeral parlor staff undressed the body that anyone noticed the woman had a bullet hole in her back?" Jake growled. "I've never seen such utter incompetence. Tell me, *Detective* Attwood, who trained you in these slipshod methods of detection?"

Attwood swallowed. "I'm new. I was at Harvard last fall when the president called on students to volunteer during the police strike," he said. "I worked for Captain Sullivan in Station Five. He was very good to us and, when the others went back, he offered me a job."

Jake's mouth dropped open. "Good God. And I suppose you being a Harvard man was enough for them to make you a detective. What in the world were they thinking?" Jake spun around and walked away, muttering to himself.

Fanny saw Attwood's shoulders slump. At least he knew he'd done wrong.

Fanny had spent the summer in New Hampshire with her daughter, returning to Boston just in time for the police strike in September. There were a few days of unrest in the city followed by months of fierce campaigning by both sides. In the end, the Police Commissioner hired fifteen hundred replacement officers and blackballed all the men who had gone out on strike. Newspapers reported that the new recruits received higher salaries and benefits, like the city paying for their uniforms. That had been one of the demands of the strikers. The city had finally conceded, but the men who had struck to get the improvements were fired and blacklisted. Newspaper stories dripped with bitterness from both sides.

Jake stopped in front of Fanny and rolled his eyes just as the boat gently docked in East Boston. All three of them, plus a driver, got into the police car and rolled off the ferry onto the shore. They drove until they were on a street with docks and wharves to their left and, on the right, brick or cement warehouses facing the street. Behind the warehouses, the rear of houses and tenements climbed a steep hill to Meridian Street above.

A few blocks down Border Street, Attwood directed the uniformed driver to turn down an alley between the Wm. H. Callahan & Son and the Sumner

Company brick buildings. At the corner, beside the Callahan warehouse, stood a pile of black iron that looked like parts of a railway bridge. In the alley, they stopped at the rear of a three-decker wooden tenement. Up the hill were more two- and three-decker tenements.

The ground floor of the house was partially blocked by an outhouse. There were trash barrels stuffed with vegetable leavings and newspapers beside a door on the right. Above were three porches with railings. On the lowest porch, Fanny saw two facing porch swings piled with rugs and blankets. Diapers and clothing were strung out on the second-floor porch, which also held an empty swing, a perambulator, and a rocking chair. The third-floor porch had lines strung for laundry, but nothing hung on them. A wooden kitchen chair stood against the rail, which was slightly broken. Fanny shivered at the thought that a woman had fallen from that porch. She estimated it was thirty feet from the porch to the ground.

Jake stood, arms akimbo as Attwood pointed up. "Mrs. Ericksson was hanging laundry on the third-floor porch. She stood on that chair to reach the line, and then she fell. Well, that's what we thought..." The young detective stumbled under Jake's angry stare. Attwood coughed. "She was found here, face down." He pointed to a spot at their feet where a few bricks and boxes were lined up to frame a bare spot. Fanny thought the people who lived there must have blocked off the space to keep from stepping on the fading bloodstains from the woman's body. She caught herself imagining the sound as the body fell through the air and landed with a thud.

Wood creaked as the mound of rugs and blankets rose from one of the first-floor porch swings.

"Jesus, Mary, and Joseph, what the hell are you people yelling about?"

Chapter Two

J ake frowned at the six-foot-five figure who rose from the first-floor
swing and cringed at the curses. He thought Fanny would likely be
offended, but it was her own fault. She had insisted on coming along.
They weren't yelling, so this big guy must have a hangover. Jake squinted.
Was that who he thought it was? "Mack? Detective McNally, is that you?"

Jake recognized the hulking police detective. He had several days' growth
of beard and wore what looked like a patrolman's long coat with one button
missing and another hanging from a thread. He wiped sleep from his eyes
with one of his big hands.

"Doc Magrath? What're you doing here?" He left his mouth slightly open.

Of course, McNally was one of the blacklisted. He would have been in the
thick of the battle over the right to unionize the police. Jake had worked with
the detective and found him competent. The man's huge size was enough to
intimidate most offenders, so he mustn't employ the brute force Jake hated to
see some of the police use. Mack was a naturally quarrelsome and contrary
character, but as far as Jake could see, that helped him be a better detective
than most. He'd question any assumption. It irritated Jake that the ignorant
Harvard boy was wearing a gold badge while Mack was sleeping it off on
the porch.

"I'm here about a death," Jake told him. He pointed at the ground. "A Mrs.
Ericksson."

Mack pursed his lips and furrowed his brow. He looked like a black storm
cloud gathering force. "She fell from the porch—or her old man slapped her
around once too many," he growled.

"She was shot through the back," Jake contradicted him. "They only found the bullet hole when they got her to Dolan's funeral home."

Mack's mouth dropped open. "No." He looked at the spot where she fell. "I'd never believe it."

Jake was frustrated. How could he do his job surrounded by such incompetence? "Were you here? Didn't you even look at her?"

Mack still looked stunned. Finally, he rubbed a hand through his dark brown hair. "No, I wasn't here. My sister told me the police said it was an accident and took her away. How could someone have shot her?" Jake could see the man was still bleary-eyed with drink as if he'd been on a bender for several days. Why not? His life was shot to hell with all this striking and blacklisting. Politics. Jake hated it.

From above, they heard a hoarse whisper. "For the love of God, will you keep it down? I've only just gotten the little ones to sleep up here, and if you wake them up again, Michael James McNally, I'll have your head on a platter."

Jake looked up and saw a tall young woman in a flowered dress covered by a white apron. He began to explain how he and the detective had returned to the place because Mrs. Erickssen had died from a gunshot, not the fall from the porch.

"Good Lord. Let me come down. I'll just shut the door so the little ones won't hear. Hush now, will you?"

When the woman came down, and through the door on the ground floor, she brought Mack with her, shooing him out to the yard in front of her. "Leave Alfie to sleep, then. He has work tonight. Not like some people." Looking up. Jake realized the second swing held a sleeping man piled up with rugs and blankets.

She was broad-shouldered for a woman, but she looked feeble beside the tall ex-detective. Nonetheless, Mack followed her directions. He had grabbed a rug, draping it over his head and round his shoulders before coming down to the yard. "Nightwatchman. You call that work. We've got to hold out for reinstatement, not give up like Alfie," he grumbled.

"A lot of chance of that. It's time you took it in like your brother. No work, no food. That union's a joke, and you know it." She gave him a shove and turned to look at Jake, Fanny, and Attwood. "I'm Catherine Gallagher, just call me Kate. I live upstairs. My husband's a fireman with Station Five. He's there more often than not. This one here," she said as she slapped Mack's shoulder, "is one of my brothers. There's five of them live in the first-floor rooms here, all McNally's. Two of them were police but got laid off in the strike."

Jake introduced himself and the others. Hunching into his rug cocoon, Mack glared at the young police detective. Jake asked about Mrs. Ericksson's death.

"I was here when Ingrid fell. It was Monday," Kate told him. "At about eleven. I was bathing one of the children; then I put him on the porch in the carriage. The other two were napping." She had three toddlers, and Jake could see she was pregnant with a fourth. She must have a strong character to manage her children, husband, and five brothers. Jake doubted he'd be able to endure her life. "I was cleaning in the kitchen when I heard the crash, so I rushed out and saw Ingrid lying on the ground. I thought she'd fallen." Kate looked worried. "The Erickssons argued a lot, but they spoke Swedish, so you didn't know what they were saying. Lars didn't always treat her right, but I never thought he pushed her. And now you're saying she was shot? But how? Who could have done that?"

Attwood stepped forward. "That's what we need to find out, Mrs. Gallagher." He looked up at the third-floor porch. "Is Mr. Ericksson home, do you know?"

"He's at work. He works for the Callahans." She pointed at the brick building beside the house. "I've got their little daughter, Lilly. I've three boys of my own, and I'm loving having the little girlie." She patted her stomach. "I'm hoping the next will be a girl for us. It's terrible sad poor little Lilly will have to grow up without her ma."

"With only that brute of a father," Mack mumbled.

Kate turned on him. "You shut your mouth. He's just a quiet man, not so noisy like your lot."

Jake was amazed to see how the big ex-police detective cowered in the face

6

of his sister's abuse. She was a woman of consequence around the tenement, that was for sure. "We'll have to go get Mr. Ericksson and let him know what really happened and that there will need to be an autopsy." Jake looked up. "Also, I'd like to look at the porch where she fell."

Mack offered to lead them to the front of the Callahan building. As they rounded the corner filled with large pieces of iron from a dissembled railway bridge, Jake sniffed the air. "What is that smell?"

The big ex-detective sniffled. "Damned if I know. They use all kinds of stuff here, I think."

Jake shook his head back and forth. "Oh, no. I know that smell. Come on. Let's find the source."

Fanny held a handkerchief to her nose, and Jake waved her back to the sidelines while he, Mack, and Attwood climbed over the iron pieces. Attwood was holding his nose with one hand. Mack shook his head at the sight, but Jake kept advancing. A big wooden storage box rested against the brick wall.

Jake grimaced at the smell, which was getting stronger. He knew what they were going to find. He supposed the wind and the corner of the building had kept the tenement residents from smelling the stink, but now it was very evident.

"Here, Mack, help me push this up." The big man hefted the unlocked top of the storage box, swearing when the smell got worse. Attwood tried to help.

"God almighty, what the hell is it?" Mack turned his face away while Attwood fell back from the box. The young detective looked green.

Jake stepped up on an iron piece to look into the box. He swept flies away as he looked down. A man's bloody body lay at the bottom.

Chapter Three

F anny felt a tug on her arm as she watched the men from the sidelines. "Don't get too close. The smell is enough to turn the stomach," Kate Gallagher said, holding a corner of her apron to her nose. Fanny thought the stench would be even more repulsive for a woman in Kate's condition. They heard Jake Magrath tell Attwood to climb into the storage bin to find out who was dead.

The young detective looked wan. He took out a clean white handkerchief and wrapped it around his nose and mouth, tying it at the back. Then he stumbled a few times, trying to climb into the box.

Mack stood with his arms crossed on his chest, still hugging the thick rug over his head and shoulders. He leaned his back against the storage box, gloating at the bumbling efforts of the young Harvard man.

Once Attwood tumbled in, he stood, and they could see the top of his red knit hat as he yelled out a description of the body. "Middle-aged, medium height, workman's clothes, and boots. His head's been smashed. It's all bloody." Attwood coughed, on the verge of heaving.

Fanny heard the woman beside her mumbling. "For the love of God…" Then Kate took a step forward and yelled. "Michael, get in there, for heaven's sake. Find out who it is. It's not one of our brothers, is it? Do something!"

The big man made a face at his sister, but he unwound himself from the rug, flinging it over the side of the storage box. With two big steps up the iron carcass of the railway bridge, he balanced on the edge of the box then jumped down. He was out of sight for a moment, then peered over the top of the box and said, "It's Conor Leary. He's been beaten to a pulp." He looked at Jake. "He works for Callahan. You'd better get someone from over there."

Jake shouted at his police driver to go get someone from the Callahan warehouse then yelled to Attwood. "Get him out of there. I'm in no fit condition to try to climb in. Get him out."

"He's one of the workmen for Bill Callahan," Kate told Fanny. "When he's not dead drunk, that is." She pulled her knitted cardigan closer around her. "That smell is disgusting, isn't it? Step back a bit."

While the women took a few steps back into the yard of the three-decker, there was commotion in the storage box and sounds of swearing. Then the corpse, rolled into Mack's rug, was slung over the side and dropped at Jake's feet. He jumped back. "Christ, what're you doing?" he yelled.

Mack pulled himself up to sit on the edge of the box with an evil grin on his face. "You wanted him out. You got him." He looked over to Attwood, who was making multiple attempts to pull himself up and out and laughed.

"Michael James McNally, get down from there and act respectful," Kate yelled. Her brother groaned and dropped to the ground, just as the policeman returned, followed by a young man in a suit with a carnation in his buttonhole. "That's Bill Callahan, the son," Kate told Fanny.

They watched as Callahan helped the young police detective down, and they rolled the body to lie face up on the rug. Jake knelt beside him. Fanny looked away from the bloody mess that was the man and was glad the sight was partially blocked.

"Dear God, yes, that's Conor," Callahan said. Then Jake huddled with him and Attwood and the uniformed man. "Yes, yes, you can use the telephone in the office," Callahan told them, and Attwood was sent away to call in reinforcements.

Kate and Fanny watched as more men in work clothes came around the corner from the Callahan building, while a single man in a three-piece suit, sucking on a pipe, hurried over from the other warehouse building.

"Ian Stewart from Sumner's," Kate told Fanny. "This'll give him something else to complain about, no doubt about it." Fanny shivered. Kate took her elbow. "Come on now, come up for a cup of tea, and let the men get at it here." She shook her head. "First Ingrid, now Conor, what's going on around here?"

Chapter Four

K ate led Fanny into the three-decker tenement and up a narrow staircase to her family apartment. She seated Fanny at a table covered with oilcloth, which stood beside a window onto the porch. Fanny could just see the corner with all the broken iron pieces. She was glad the view of the storage bin was blocked.

It was a small kitchen piled with supplies and dishes. A brass tub was filled with soapy water and clothes. Kate must have been washing diapers when the excitement began. After setting a kettle on the stove, the sturdy woman pulled out some wet cloths, wrung them out, and stepped out to the porch to hang them from the lines strung across. She was tall enough to fling them over and use a wooden peg to keep them on the line. The wind was blocked, so the laundry only swung gently.

"Warmed up some?" Kate asked as she returned to the kitchen. She filled a teapot and put two mugs on the table, filling them after the tea had barely steeped. "Take that." She handed a mug to Fanny. The porcelain felt hot in Fanny's hands, and she appreciated the warmth.

When Kate sat down, pinning back some threads of hair that had broken loose in the cold wind, Fanny recognized the signs in the other woman as she bent forward over her own mug. Kate was ready for a good gossip. "The man they found was named Conor Leary?" Fanny asked.

Kate took a big gulp of the hot tea. "No milk or sugar, I'm sorry to say. But this tastes good anyhow, doesn't it? Aye, that was Conor Leary. His wife left him last year. She'd had enough of the drinking and all. But Bill Callahan keeps him on. Uses him as a messenger. Bill's always doing favors for the

Dems, the democratic ward men. Not that it's only them he's close with. You should see him hang on the coattails of the old Yank. He's an up-and-coming man."

"He owns the company?"

"No, actually, his da started it. Old William was a ship's carpenter and worked for Donald McKay, the man who had the big shipyard, built all the fast ships that sailed to China and so forth. But William Callahan senior left McKay twenty-five years ago to start his own company. They build docks, wharves, bridges, tunnels. But Old William isn't a man about town like the young one. He'd rather hunker down with working men, like Lars, upstairs. They play chess and sip aquavit." She shook her head in wonder at the absurdities of men.

Fanny realized that Kate would be a fount of information about the people in the three-decker. "Lars, that's Lars Ericksson, the husband of the woman who died?"

"That's it. That's right. He's a big Swede. He's a ship's carpenter like Old William started out as. He works for the Callahan company, too. They don't do ships, but there's plenty of carpenter work on their jobs. Old William really took to him, even though his English is not so good sometimes. But I think the old man is closer to him than to his own son. There's another Callahan son, too, but he's in the Navy, and he's still out in France now."

Fanny could see the woman was settling down for a good talk. She spoke softly so as not to wake the napping children, and she kept glancing out the window to keep track of the men, but she was quite cozy, sitting with Fanny. She eyed the fur coat and hat with some curiosity but seemed content to provide information before starting an interrogation of Fanny. Whatever she found out would be sure to be fodder for more gossip after Fanny left.

"Do you have any idea who could have shot Mrs. Ericksson?" Fanny asked. She needed to strike while the iron was hot before Kate counter-attacked with her own questions.

"No, never. Shot! Who'd have thought? We all thought she fell, hanging out laundry. She wasn't all that friendly, to tell the truth. She was sent over from the small town in Sweden that they came from. Somewhere in the south where they've got lots of boats and harbors. She and Lars married and had Lilly, the daughter, last year. I love that little girl; she's a darlin'.

"Anyhow, like I said, she wasn't all that friendly, and then, they're Lutherans." Kate wrinkled her nose at that, like the religion was some sort of strange spice. "So, they didn't go to Most Holy Redeemer, like us." She paused and looked into space, warming her hands on her tea mug. "Ingrid's English wasn't so good. I'd say a word to her, and she'd just nod, like she understood, even when she didn't. She knew how to ask me to watch Lilly for her, though. She could speak pretty well then."

"Did her husband really beat her?" Fanny asked. She was getting a picture of the dead woman that would be important to Jake and the police. Fanny hoped it would make Jake see how useful she could be in investigations.

Kate shook herself. "Oh, that's Mack talkin' about Lars slappin' her around. They certainly argued a lot, but in Swedish. I only ever heard of him hittin' her once. She was a bit of a flirt, that one. She might not be able to talk to me, but I'd see her talkin' to Bill Callahan when he came for his da, or to my brothers, downstairs. She was the kind who had no time for other women, if you know what I mean."

"Was she pretty?"

Kate snorted. "Pretty all right, blond braids pinned up, a nice figure. Always pretty dresses, too. Lars kept her well."

"And Lars, what's he like?"

"Good looking, too. A big, tall blond Swede. But he's the quiet, brooding type. Good at his job, though. I think Ian was trying to lure him away from Callahan."

"Ian? He was the man smoking the pipe?"

"Yes. Ian Stewart, Scottish. He works for the Sumner company across the alley. They build docks and bridges and such, too. Compete with Callahan for government contracts like. But that's an old Yankee company, descended from one of the men who first bought land here. You won't see Augustus Lane Sumner, the current owner, around often. Spends his time on Beacon Hill or in Marblehead. Ian runs the place for him. Mack says he's Sumner's lapdog, but he's just jealous." She shook her head. "This strike just ruined it all for Mack and Alfie. At least Alfie's getting on with his life. Mack is one big heavy stuck rock, drinking himself to oblivion, like that would cure anything for him."

There was a cry from the other room. "They'll be waking," Kate said. She rose but, before leaving, she leaned over and pulled aside the curtain on the window. "Look, they're coming back."

Chapter Five

Standing in the cold, Jake gave instructions to the ambulance men to take the body of Conor Leary to the morgue on North Grove Street. He'd have his work cut out for him when he got back, with both Leary and the Ericksson woman's bodies to work on. Detective Attwood was still inside, talking to his superiors on the telephone. Mack had grabbed a chair and was picking his teeth with a letter opener while he watched the inexperienced detective. Frustrated, Jake had led the ambulance men to the body. Attwood was useless.

Jake hoped his assistant Edwin would be back from his classes. After the murder case the past year, Jake had gotten Edwin enrolled in medical studies at Harvard. He was a former army medic who had been badly burned in the war. Jake used his influence as a graduate and a current part-time professor to get Edwin into the program. It was inconvenient not to have his assistant with him on calls like this, but he was proud of the young man's progress and knew the medical examiner's office would benefit in the long run.

Looking around, Jake realized Fanny had disappeared. She must be inside the three-decker. He would bet she'd made friends with Kate Gallagher. He'd better find her.

Fanny had shown up in Boston after her summer in New Hampshire eager to continue their association that had led them to solve a murder the previous winter. After that case, he'd shared his frustration with the way police investigators were trained and, in a fit of imagination, had suggested she could help him formulate training for them. Fanny was like a dog with a bone, and she wasn't going to let go of the idea. He had some doubts as to his own sanity in making the suggestion but, with Edwin away so much, he saw no harm in bringing her along to take notes. Certainly, Peter Attwood, even if he had gone to Harvard, had a lot to learn.

Before Jake could trudge over to the back door, Bill Callahan showed up with a tall blond-haired man who he introduced as Lars Ericksson, husband of the woman who fell to her death after being shot. Callahan hurried back to his office as Jake shook the grieving man's hand.

By the time they reached the three-decker, Fanny was waiting in the yard. Jake turned to the tall man following him. "Fanny, this is Mr. Lars Ericksson. He's the husband of Ingrid Ericksson. I've asked him to let us look at the porch where she fell."

The big Swede nodded and stepped ahead to lead them up the internal stairs to the third-floor apartment. Jake felt good that he didn't huff and puff at all on his climb up the stairs. The constant exercise rowing all summer and fall helped keep him in shape. He was a good dozen years older than Fanny but took pride in his physical abilities.

Inside, the three rooms were small but neat. Jake noted an oil painting of a harbor in golden sunshine hanging in the small parlor. He wondered if it was the town Ericksson and his wife had come from. The furniture was sparse but sturdy, carved from light wood. Perhaps the ship's carpenter had built them himself. The cushions looked as if they were hand embroidered with ships and anchors in the patterns.

The long-faced Swede led them into a small kitchen with a wood-burning stove, quartered logs stacked neatly in a basket beside it. Pots and pans hung from hooks under the shelves on the walls. They went through a door onto the porch.

Lars Ericksson winced as he pointed to the wooden kitchen chair placed under the laundry lines and the partly broken railing beside it. He covered his face with his hand and ducked back into the kitchen. Jake knew it must be difficult for the man to relive the catastrophe everyone thought was an accident. Fanny stared at the chair.

Jake reached out and felt the chair. It rocked a bit, uneven on the floor of the porch. "No wonder they thought she fell by accident," he said. He bent over the rail, looking down. "We need to measure how far the body was from the side of the house. And look at that." He pointed to an empty window box on the second-floor porch that had been knocked off on one side so it hung off-kilter. "She must have hit that on the way down."

Fanny pulled out a pad of paper and began sketching.

"Oh, good," Jake said. He liked her initiative. Making drawings of the scene was something even Edwin wouldn't be capable of. Using Fanny as an assistant might have some benefits after all. He remembered the miniature room that was a copy of the scene of the crime she had created the previous year. That skill could be helpful, too.

"Good idea," he told her. "Be sure to get the whole scene from down there, too."

She raised an eyebrow at him and flipped back a page of the pad to show how she had already done a sketch of the back of the building.

He shrugged and left her drawing to go back into the kitchen, where Lars Ericksson was seated at a plain but beautiful little round table. He had a bottle of liquor and two small glasses in front of him. His head was in his hands.

Jake seated himself. "I'm sorry to have to tell you this, Mr. Ericksson, but we have discovered that your wife's death was not an accident."

Lars looked up red-eyed and stared at Jake with incomprehension. Jake hoped his English was good enough to understand. "Please tell me what happened when your wife fell from the porch."

"I told police."

"I know, but please tell me again." Jake had introduced himself as the medical examiner, but he wasn't sure the man understood what that meant.

Lars sighed. "I was in the kitchen." He spoke slowly. "My wife did laundry for the week. Ingrid was on the porch. She stood on the chair. She hung laundry. Suddenly, I heard a sound. Not sure what it was. I looked out. She's not there. I go out, look down, she's on the ground below." His eyes rose to the ceiling as if looking for an answer, then he dropped his face into his hands again. "She fell," he murmured.

"That's what everyone thought, but actually, she was shot. In the back."

Lars's head snapped up. "Shot? What do you mean?"

Jake nodded. "Yes, I'm sorry, but she was shot. I'll be conducting an autopsy to clarify what happened as much as possible. Apparently, no one noticed until the funeral home people undressed the body. They found the bullet hole. So, she didn't just fall. She was shot."

Lars shook his head. "Impossible."

"Didn't you hear the shot?"

"No, no."

"Do you own a gun?" Jake thought Detective Attwood ought to be the one asking these questions, but the inexperienced young man was overwhelmed with the discovery of a second body, and Jake didn't want to wait for what would probably be a less-than-competent interrogation by the official detective. More than once that day, he'd thought Mack ought to be doing this. At least he had experience.

"Gun. Yes. Small rifle only. Use it for rabbits in the country."

"Rabbits. All right." Jake had a tickle at the back of his mind, warning him that if this husband had shot his wife, then being alone with him while demanding to see his gun might not be the most intelligent thing to do. He was mindful of Fanny out on the porch. What if the man turned violent?

Jake stepped out onto the porch. Looking down, he saw Mack trudging across the yard.

"Mack, Detective McNally," Jake yelled, hoping the use of the title would be flattering. "Can you come up here for a moment? We might need your help."

Fanny was looking at Jake with a question on the tip of her tongue, but he ignored her and went back inside. "We'll need to borrow your gun to examine it," he told Lars.

"Borrow?"

It was like talking to an echo. "Yes. Just get it, will you?"

Lars went to a cupboard in the hallway. Returning, he lumbered into the room, holding a comparatively small rifle. Jake judged it to be .22 caliber. He pointed to the table, and Lars put the gun down. Jake could hear Mack pounding up the stairs, and the big Irishman loomed in the doorway just as

Fanny stepped in from the porch.

Mack looked a question at Jake, then he eyed the tall Swede. Lars looked confused, not roused or angry. Jake glanced at Fanny. He hoped she was done with her sketching because he had an urge to get out of this house.

"Mack, Lars has shown us his rifle. Would you be so good as to take it and come down to the motorcar with us? Fanny, it's time to leave. I need to get back to the morgue for the autopsies." He shooed Fanny ahead of him to the stairs. Mack took up the rifle from the table, checking it carefully to make sure it wasn't loaded. He nodded to Lars, who stood with his mouth open as the trio fled down the stairs.

In the yard, Attwood was just turning the corner from the Callahan building. "They've taken the body away to your morgue." He looked pale. "What do we do now?"

Mack snorted.

Jake led the way to the police car. "Now we cut open the bodies to see what they can tell us." Out of the corner of his eye, he saw the detective pale even more.

Fanny looked like she wanted to scold Jake for shocking the young detective.

Mack laughed.

Chapter Six

It took longer than Jake expected to get the ferry back to the North End. Mack had hitched a ride with them, saying he had a meeting at committee headquarters that evening. Jake thought the big ex-detective was gloating over Attwood's obvious incompetence. Unfortunately, the way things worked in the city, Mack was unlikely to get his job back. It irked Jake that Mack was off the force while Attwood and more politically savvy old detectives remained.

At the North Grove Street mortuary, the body of Conor Leary had not yet arrived. Jake assumed they'd taken the long way round instead of the ferry. Access to East Boston was always awkward. So near and yet so far, just across the inner harbor from the North End, but with no bridge and only a streetcar tunnel.

He was pleased to find Edwin in the laboratory where he had laid out Ingrid Ericksson's body under a white sheet. Jake and Fanny hung their coats and piled their things in Jake's office. Attwood's eyes bulged, and he couldn't seem to take his gaze away from the shrouded body. He gulped. "Dr. Magrath, do you need me here for this?"

Jake was surprised. Was the young detective really so ignorant of procedure? Mack had slouched into the room behind Attwood, and he dropped into a wooden chair by the wall, amused by Attwood's ignorance. Jake decided to allow Mack to stay, even if it was a little unorthodox since the ex-detective had no standing in the current investigation. At least Mack knew the procedures, for heaven's sake.

"It's customary for the detective in charge to observe," Jake told him as

Edwin helped him into an all-encompassing white apron. "It's not required, however, if you'd rather not." He watched as Attwood saw Fanny draw up a chair at the foot of the gurney, pulling out her notepad and pencil.

"I'll stay," Attwood said. Clearly, he didn't want to be put to shame by a mere woman. He looked around, but there were only the two occupied chairs, so he was forced to stand. Jake gently pulled the sheet off the young woman's body.

Mack gasped and put a big hand over his face. Of course, he had known the woman when she was alive and, despite the experienced detective's hardened exterior, Jake could see he was moved by the sight of the dead woman.

She was pretty. The skin was beginning to desiccate from two days of dehydration, but Jake could see she had light blue eyes, long lashes, and silky blond hair escaping from braids pinned around her head in a sort of halo. Her nose was slightly turned up, and she had pink lips. The funeral home had washed away the blood from gashes on the face and front of the body where she had fallen face first. Jake guessed she must have collided with the broken flowerbox on the first-floor porch on the way down, then hit some small rocks on the ground.

Jake walked around the table to her right side and pushed up the shoulder. Edwin held her as Jake examined the bullet hole. Again, the funeral home had already washed away any blood. He gently pushed at the wound and felt the front abdomen, searching for a sign of the bullet. He found an exit wound in the front of the woman's body.

"We'll have to find the bullet. Edwin, let her back down, and we'll start at the front." Jake moved to the other side of the table and chose a scalpel. He glanced up and saw Attwood was even paler than before. Jake glared at Mack. The big man stood and took the young detective by the shoulders, sitting him down in the chair. "Can't have you fainting away now, darlin'" Mack said.

Even the jaded older detective was solemn despite the jest. Jake felt a cloud of sadness descend on the room. Such a young and lovely woman, so very gone from the world. It wasn't fair. But it was a long time since Jake had expected fairness from the world. He'd seen a lot of tragedy, but what kept him going was the search for truth.

Jake took a big breath. In his work, he found that rigid objectivity in method, a mind free from prejudgment, an ear deaf to theorizing were needed. Sooner or later, truth would crystallize from the mass of facts they would accumulate concerning this young woman's death. Before he made the first incision, it occurred to him that Fanny, more than the men present, seemed determined to clarify the truth of what had happened, rather than to pity the poor girl on the table. Sometimes, women shocked him with their acceptance of unpleasant realities. The men saw what might have been for the lovely young girl. Fanny saw she was dead, and her death required an explanation.

Chapter Seven

F anny was satisfied with her participation in the investigation so far. She had drawn meticulous sketches of the three-decker and the yard of the Callahan company. She had gotten useful information from Kate Gallagher about the people who lived there, and she had recorded Jake's observations during the autopsy. She would turn them into a typed report the following day. Jake required written reports at every step of the investigation into the cause and manner of death. The reports would be filed with the district attorney and with the court of jurisdiction if criminal actions or negligence were found. She also knew those reports could be used if Jake determined a reconstruction was necessary to get at the facts of the case. She was thinking a reconstruction would be needed in this case, and she remembered the miniature she'd created the previous winter, which had helped to solve the case. She was anxious to try her hand at that kind of reconstruction again. She'd been thinking of that when she made her drawings at the site.

She was mulling over all of this as she walked up the back side of Beacon Hill and down to Louisburg Square after the autopsy of Ingrid Ericksson. Conor Leary's body had finally been delivered, but Jake had put off that autopsy to the next day. Realizing that Edwin's classes in Cambridge would conflict, Jake had asked Fanny to attend to take notes. She felt like she was really getting a foothold in the work she wanted to do with Jake.

Dead leaves crackled on the brick walk as she passed the sedate rowhouses that surrounded the little park. She was lucky that her friend Cornelia Thornwell had insisted she stay in a guest room of her Beacon Hill mansion when she came back to Boston. Cornelia was a petite, elderly woman with a modest demeanor that hid a revolutionary heart. She had introduced Fanny to suffragists, civil reformers, and other radicals hiding beneath the gentrified exterior of the Boston Brahmin culture. Fanny was grateful to her.

Besides which, Cornelia was fun. She was as uninterested in the latest fashions, in dress or furnishings as Fanny. She was fully capable of supporting Fanny's fiction that she was remaining in Boston to purchase antiques, rugs, and designer porcelain, while involving her in various more interesting activities. And she had tickets to the Symphony and other cultural institutions that Fanny genuinely liked to visit. Fanny felt more comfortable in Cornelia's version of society than she was in her mother's version back in Chicago. She knew it was probably because of the divorce that she herself had instigated. Her parents supported her choice, but she knew they weren't entirely comfortable with it, and she didn't really want to meet her ex-husband on social occasions. That wouldn't happen in Boston.

She hopped up the steep stone stairs to the front door, which was opened by Cornelia's butler, Harris.

"Mrs. Thornwell is in the parlor with her grandson," he told her. "She has tea served there, and she said you're welcome to join them." He took Fanny's coat and hat and laid her case on a table by the mirror.

"Thank you. I'll do that."

Harris opened the tall door on the right, and she walked into a spacious room with a roaring fire. Cushioned chairs were pulled up to a low table, which held a teapot, cups, and a serving plate of small sandwiches and pastries. Cornelia greeted her and remained sitting, pulling up a teacup to pour for Fanny. The young man opposite her stood politely to be introduced, and Fanny realized he was Detective Attwood. They stared at each other with dismay.

Chapter Eight

"Mrs. Lee." A blush spread from the young detective's neck to his forehead.

Cornelia looked up. "Fanny, have you already met my grandson? Peter, you've met Mrs. Lee before?" She looked happy, but she noticed embarrassment in the air and cocked her head. "Exactly how did you meet?"

Fanny sat on one of the cushioned chairs, reaching for her cup. Young Attwood looked flummoxed. She took pity on him. "I went on a call with Dr. Magrath this morning, and Detective Attwood was the primary investigator. I had no idea you had a policeman with a gold badge in the family." She watched Attwood recover a little and take his seat.

"I'm afraid Mrs. Lee didn't see me at my best," he said. "I've totally ruined everything already." He looked glum, waving away a tray of cakes from his grandmother.

"Oh, come on, I'm sure it's not that bad," Cornelia said. She turned to Fanny. "Peter left Harvard and joined the police force out of concern for civic reform. I'm very proud of him."

Attwood slumped in his chair. "The rest of the family aren't. Wait till my father hears how I've messed up. He'll gloat about it."

Without the bulky knit hat, mittens, and scarf, Fanny could see that Peter Attwood was a gangly young man with light brown hair that was a bit long and sideburns. His face had a long nose and light blue eyes that looked worried. He wore a gray suit of very fine wool with white cuffs and collar and a silk tie. He looked at home in the warm, gentle firelight of Cornelia's parlor with her paper-thin porcelain teacups and generous milk and sugar. Compared to Kate Gallagher's thick mugs and chilly kitchen, Cornelia's house was a different world. Fanny herself was becoming accustomed to visiting both sides of the dividing line between the wealthy Brahmin and the hardscrabble immigrant communities. It must be just as jarring for a young man like Peter Attwood.

After a sip, Fanny set down her cup and saucer. Peter seemed unwilling to expand on the story. Painful as it might be, it would be best to get the story out and learn from it. She turned to Cornelia. "A woman's body was found yesterday in East Boston. They assumed she'd died from a fall. She was hanging laundry on the porch."

"*I* assumed," Peter grumbled.

"Yes. So, the body was delivered to the undertakers, but when they undressed her, they found a bullet wound. She was shot."

Peter closed his eyes and groaned. "I should have seen the bullet wound when we found her. There was blood, but it looked like she bled from the injuries she got in the fall. She was a mess. The Chief Detective took one look and told me to hurry up and move on to another problem back in the North End. I should have looked more closely."

Peter grasped his knees. "Dr. Magrath was furious this morning when the funeral home called him about the mistake. I'm not sure if I'll still have a job after this, and I'm already off the books at Harvard. My father will be gleeful. And you, Granny, after all your support, you'll be so disappointed. What a fool I've been."

Cornelia reached over to pat his hand. "Surely they know you're new to the job and will consider it part of your training," she said.

Fanny scoffed. "I'll bet your superior officer was none too happy to have a young Harvard man assigned to him, was he, Peter?"

Fanny knew the young man's chief inspector was probably an Irish cop from the old guard who would resent a Harvard man. There was some sort of infinite divide between the Brahmins and the immigrant populations in Boston. It was different in kind from the divisions in her native Chicago. It was much more blatant and irrevocable, like a fissure in the earth that was too wide to be crossed. You were on one side or the other. It seemed to her that young Peter Attwood had unwittingly crossed over to the side where he didn't belong. But somehow, Jake Magrath managed to command respect from both sides of that border.

Cornelia was looking at her grandson with pity. "Poor Peter. Are you thinking of quitting?"

He stood up and moved restlessly to the fireplace. "I don't know. If I do, Father will insist I return to Harvard and then join the bank to toil away behind a desk for the rest of my life. It's not fair. I don't want to work at the bank. I hate the idea. The first time I ever felt I could actually do something in the world was when I was helping to protect the peace during the strike last fall. I know there's corruption in the city; I'm not naive, but Captain Sullivan wasn't like that. He was hard, but fair, and he knew how to deploy the men and handle the crowds, so no one got hurt. I admire him. I think policing and keeping order is important work. More than counting money in a chilly stone building." Having had his say, he sat down again.

"Too bad you're not working for Captain Sullivan," Cornelia said. "Perhaps there's some way to get you transferred."

"No. You can't interfere. Don't you see that's half the trouble? It was the higher-ups, probably Mayor Peters and Commissioner Curtis, who saw a Harvard man on the roster and gave me a detective's badge. I'm from Beacon Hill. I'm one of them. Imagine how that looks to men who've been patrolling the streets and working hard jobs. Any of the old-guard that are still there have political pull. Curtis might want to get rid of them, but he can't. It's a big thing to get a gold badge, and I came in off the street and was handed one. That's the problem, right there. To have some influential relative or friend get me transferred after I screwed up on my first homicide would just make things worse. I don't know what I'm going to do. I was a fool to think I could do this job."

Fanny thought it was a tragedy that both Peter Attwood and Mack McNally could be driven from their jobs while someone with political connections remained on the force. Jake was frustrated by the quality of police investigations already. The current situation after the police strike would only make it worse.

"What if you solve this murder investigation?" she asked. "Wouldn't that fix your problem?"

Peter snorted. "I suppose. I don't know how we'll find out who shot the woman, and now there's another body, and I have no idea who beat that man to death."

Fanny explained to Cornelia how they'd found the body of Conor Leary in the storage bin. Cornelia clenched her teeth at the image. She had obviously encouraged her grandson in his rebellion against his father's plans for him, but she might be doubting the wisdom of that action now. Peter could have been safe at his studies over in Cambridge rather than finding decomposing bodies in noxious places like the warehouses of East Boston.

Fanny knew the town of Cambridge, across the Charles River from Beacon Hill, was another bastion of Brahmin culture. But East Boston, like the North End and South Boston, was crowded with new immigrants from Ireland, Italy, and Eastern Europe. There seemed to be invisible lines between the ethnic communities. Cross them and you were in a foreign country.

The fierce distinctions weren't necessary, in Fanny's opinion. She didn't think Cornelia's grandson would be happy back at Harvard now that he'd had a taste of something more immediate and exciting, and Jake would be deprived of an eager, intelligent student if he quit. She knew the medical examiner longed to train police detectives in proper death investigation techniques. The plan to train investigators had brought her back to Boston. Why not start with Detective Attwood? She wanted to offer him an alternative. "You could work closely with Dr. Magrath on these deaths. He knows you're inexperienced. But he's deeply dissatisfied with how police work in death investigations as it is. If you work with him, I'm sure he'd want to teach you better methods."

Peter sighed. "He didn't seem like he had much patience with me today. He wanted to bite my head off from the beginning. He thinks I'm incompetent. And he's right. I don't know how to go about finding the murderer or murderers. It's hopeless."

"Don't they give you any training?" Cornelia asked.

Peter's shoulders drooped, like a deflated balloon. "No. I just follow the Chief Detective and take orders from him. I don't know what I'm doing."

Fanny wouldn't accept that. "Facts. You have to collect facts, lay them out, and let them lead you to the right conclusion." She'd learned that much in her work with Jake so far. "Listen, Dr. Magrath has done plenty of investigations where he's found the guilty party. He testifies in murder trials all the time. He knows how to solve a murder, and he knows how *not* to go about it. Work with him. He'll find out what happened. You'll see."

"I want to be a detective," Peter said. "It's not just that I want to prove my father wrong about me. I want to do something worthwhile with my life. Finding the truth in a murder investigation is important. If we can separate the wheat from the chaff, the chaff can be removed from society so that ordinary people can live their lives. That's what I want to do."

Cornelia sat back and looked at her grandson. "Then, I think you will need to persevere, Peter. You know I will support you."

"Even if no one else does," he said, frowning.

Fanny sipped her tea. She hoped she'd done the right thing. She knew her own ambition was driving her to want her friend's grandson to persevere. Jake could teach this young man the correct way to investigate. And Fanny could help him do it.

Chapter Nine

When Jake reached the door of the North Grove Street Mortuary the next morning, he found Mack waiting for him. The big ex-policeman must have been up early to catch a ferry from East Boston and arrive by eight o'clock. He'd obviously been home as he was clean-shaven, his dark hair plastered back with hair oil. He wore a navy peacoat with all the buttons intact, unlike his coat from the day before, which had needed repair. Jake frowned. "What are you doing here so early?"

Mack shrugged. "I want to help." He recognized skepticism in Jake's face, so he hurried on. "Ingrid Ericksson died at our house. My sister lives there. We need to know what happened and that we're safe. Besides, at least I knew Conor Leary. Come on, Doc. You know that young Harvard boy is going to have to talk to the men at the Callahan company. Do you think they'll tell him anything? A little smart-ass Yankee whippersnapper, like that? They'll talk to me."

Jake stopped and considered him. He wasn't sure why Mack was so intent on forcing his way into the investigation. Officially, he was no longer a police detective. On the other hand, Jake had reservations about Detective Attwood's competence. He shook his head at the dilemma. Something was driving Mack to interfere, but Jake didn't believe he was involved in the deaths. More likely, he was in despair over the loss of a job he loved and was good at. Perhaps he was looking for a way to accomplish something while his union continued its doomed fight to get his job back for him. Jake unlocked the door.

"You won't be in charge, and you'll have to stop needling Attwood. But, if you want to help, I'm not going to stop you. Come on in."

He led the way into the main autopsy room. Before leaving for his classes in Cambridge, Edwin had prepared Conor Leary's body, but he left a note saying he'd returned the body to refrigeration. Jake continued on to his office, and when he returned, Fanny and Peter Attwood had arrived. He cleared his throat. "Former Detective McNally, Mack here, has offered to assist in this investigation, and I think it's a good idea." He looked at Peter. The young detective looked worried. He stared at the sheet-covered body as if steeling himself. And he bit his lip. Jake guessed that he wasn't looking forward to his second autopsy but, if he wanted to be a police detective, he'd have to get used to it.

Fanny settled herself with a notepad and pencil. "That will be useful, don't you think, Detective Attwood? After all, Detective McNally knows the people since he lives there."

Jake noticed that Peter didn't reply. Probably, he was too wrapped up in his own thoughts and fears. But Mack preened himself. Obviously, he liked hearing Fanny refer to him as a detective. She knew how to stroke a young man's ego. Jake scrutinized Fanny and Peter. Something was different. Why was Fanny patronizing the young man she'd met only the day before?

Pulling on his apron and gloves, he dismissed the question. He had more important things to deal with. He handed out face masks. "I'll bring the Leary body from cold storage, but I have to warn you the smell will be unpleasant."

Mack and Peter had experienced the smell the day before, but they'd just have to suffer it again if they wanted to witness the autopsy. Jake noticed Mack stuff paper in his nostrils. Peter looked sick already, and Fanny looked determined. So be it.

Jake wheeled in the body under a white sheet. Edwin had placed the clothes in a bag at the foot of the stretcher. Jake recalled a friend from medical school who described the smell of putrefaction as "dense, wet, and shockingly sweet like the vomit of a drunk." The stench seeped into the room. Most bodies Jake autopsied were fresh and kept cold enough to slow decay, but he'd dealt with enough older bodies to ignore the smell.

He began with a simple description of the height, weight, sex, and general condition. Leary was a man in his fifties and in pretty good shape for a lifetime of hard work. Fanny dutifully wrote out each comment. Peter had retreated behind a wooden chair, and he clutched the back throughout the procedure. Mack paced around, stepping over to look when Jake pointed out any unusual finding.

After an hour, the organs had been removed and weighed, the body rotated more than once, and a dozen pages of Fanny's notebook were filled. They'd become accustomed to the smell and to Mack's harsh sounds as he breathed through his mouth.

When Jake began sewing up the incisions in the dead man's chest, he asked, "So, what have we learned?" He wondered if they'd understood anything.

Mack stopped his pacing and gestured to Peter. Jake looked up.

Peter cleared his throat. "Conor Leary was beaten to death. Someone struck him repeatedly on the head and shoulders."

"Yes," Jake said, and he saw the young detective take a big breath. He must be used to examinations at Harvard. He hoped Peter wasn't just guessing the answer. Jake took the head in his hands. "He was struck in the back of the head, here."

"From behind," Mack said, unable to contain himself.

"Probably. He fell down, face first, and his attacker struck four more blows to the back of his head. They fractured his skull."

"Clubbed him while he was down to make sure he was dead," Mack said.

"I see." Peter bent to examine the wounds. At least he was paying attention.

Jake pointed at the middle of the body. "Here, there are three broken ribs. But note there is no bruising. Does that tell us anything?"

Peter frowned.

"He was dead when the ribs broke," Mack said.

Jake sighed. Lack of experience would hamper this investigation. He shook his head at the thought of the politicians who thought giving a gold badge to a Harvard boy was the right move. The young man really needed Mack's help.

"Why would you hit a man in the ribs when he was already dead?" Peter asked and Jake was glad that at least he was thinking.

Mack blew air out of his lips. "He broke the ribs, getting the body into the bin." Mack stood and mimed picking up a body, heaving it over the side of a bin, and then tipping the legs up to push it in. Jake could see the action. "Broke the ribs when he balanced the body on the edge. That would happen if it was one man doing it. If there were two of them, they could heave him over without breaking the ribs." He was very pleased with himself. Peter sighed in despair. Jake was pretty sure the young detective was used to being the smartest one in the room. He hated that Mack was ahead of him. From Jake's point of view, it might not be a bad thing to promote the competition. They needed results.

Mack asked the logical next question. "When was he killed?"

"Based on the degree of decay, the smell, and the insects, I'd say he's about three to four days gone," Jake said. It was like spoiled meat. He decided it was time for a lesson.

"Fanny, you don't have to take this down. This is just for the edification of you all. When a person dies, rigor sets in after about three hours." He saw Mack nod. He'd dealt with stiff-as-a-board corpses. "After about twenty-four hours, rigor subsides. Mr. Leary was no longer stiff. After twenty-four to seventy-two hours, the internal organs decompose, and you get the pungent odors we're smelling. Three to five days after, bodily fluid starts leaking out, and the skin turns green. Mr. Leary hasn't reached that point. Later, the body turns red, the teeth and nails fall out, and finally, the body liquefies, leaving only the skeleton."

Gruesome but true. Fanny stared into the room, unseeing. The facts led to ruminations on mortality. Fanny was contemplating death. Jake saw it in his medical students all the time. But to his surprise, Peter perked up.

"Was Leary killed at the same time as Ingrid Ericksson then? Or before her? Perhaps she saw something, and that's why she's dead."

Jake liked that the detective was turning away from brooding to fit the facts to his investigation. Before he could answer, Mack spoke up.

"No. Conor was alive when Ingrid fell from the porch. He was in the crowd around her. I saw him."

Chapter Ten

Fanny could see that the ex-policeman enjoyed throwing the discussion off with his revelation. In her estimation, Mack was insufferable. But he was experienced. And Cornelia's grandson was not. Peter looked tongue-tied. On the other hand, she wondered if Mack was too close to the situation. Should he be involved in the investigation? "Were you present when Mrs. Ericksson fell from the porch?" she asked.

"No. I was away at the pub, but when I came back, there was a crowd around Ingrid. Poor, poor girl."

"If Leary was there, she wasn't killed because she knew about his murder, but perhaps the other way around," Jake said. "Maybe he saw something. Who else was there?"

"Wouldn't he have spoken up, if he saw who did it?" Peter asked. Fanny was glad he was questioning the facts. She wanted to urge him on.

Mack snorted. "Not if he could've got something by not speaking up. Leary was a drunk. They only kept him on because he'd been with the Callahan company for a long time. He was a slippery bastard. Excuse my French, ma'am."

Fanny took no offense, but she distrusted the ex-detective.

"Who else was there?" Jake repeated.

"Everybody by then. Kate, her husband, two of my brothers, more of the gang from the Callahan works, including young Bill Callahan, even a few from the Sumner building. Ian Stewart, nosy bugger that he is. And that oaf, Lars, was slobbering over her."

Fanny remembered the area in the back of the three-decker where the body had been found. It made sense that people living in the building would have gathered around the woman, including Mack's relatives and Lars Ericksson, the dead woman's husband. Staff from the Callahan and Sumner warehouses that stood between the scene of the death and Border Street would also be alerted.

Fanny realized Mack had strong opinions about the people in East Boston. She wondered if that bias would influence an investigation. Jake insisted an objective approach to the facts was essential. It annoyed her that Jake let the ex-detective make such comments about Lars Ericksson and the Sumner manager, Ian Stewart, without correction.

"So, what's next, Detective Attwood?" Jake asked.

Peter shuffled away from the dead body. He glanced at Fanny as if looking for help. She couldn't help him. He needed to face Jake on his own. She bit her lip, hoping he'd succeed.

Peter coughed and straightened up. "Interview the people Leary worked with. Talk to the people who knew Mrs. Ericksson."

Jake frowned. "Aren't you forgetting something?"

Peter stared at him with his mouth partially open.

"The weapon, you idiot. We must have missed it in that storage bin or somewhere around the yard," Mack told Peter sarcastically. Fanny found him offensive. She opened her mouth, prepared to rebuke him, but Jake motioned for her to remain quiet.

"That's right," Jake said. "You need to locate the weapon used to pummel Leary. But you also need to talk to the people you mentioned."

Peter's ears had turned red. Fanny thought he purposely avoided looking at Mack who was pacing back and forth in front of the body, like a horse anxious to gallop. She worried that he'd bully young Peter if they were sent off together. Surely Jake must see it would be a disaster?

"I talked to Mrs. Gallagher yesterday," Fanny said, hoping to change the subject. She told them what Kate had said. Careful to avoid spreading gossip about the dead woman, Fanny told them that Kate had suggested Ingrid was a flirt. "She mentioned the younger Mr. Callahan as someone Mrs. Ericksson might have flirted with."

Mack grunted. "No. Don't listen to female gossip. Ingrid had nothing to do with Bill Callahan. He just came over all the time to get his father away from her husband. If anybody hurt Ingrid, it was that Swedish bump on a log of a husband."

Fanny felt heat rise to her cheeks. The man had downright contradicted her, and Jake was letting him get away with it. Female gossip, indeed. Male jealousy, more likely.

Peter spoke up. "It's worth asking about Mrs. Ericksson's, ah, relationships with the other men in the area." Before Mack could argue, Peter hurried on. "Even if it's not true, if her husband heard such gossip, it might have given him a reason to be jealous."

Mack's brow furrowed, and Fanny expected an outbreak of insults, but Jake intervened. "Good point, Detective Attwood. That's one of a number of things you should pursue."

That exchange prevented Mack from disputing with Peter. Fanny suspected he feared Jake would remove him from the investigation if he didn't behave. She didn't know why Jake had included him anyway.

Mack licked his lips. "Callahan has been having some unexplained accidents," he told them. "Some damage to a wharf they were building and some thefts from work sites. It's been happening a lot in the last month. Sometimes more than once a week."

This was news. Obviously, Mack's knowledge of the background in the neighborhood was relevant. And he knew how to think about a situation like this. She was beginning to see why Jake wanted him to work with Peter.

"That's a thread to follow," Jake told him. "Now, Detective Attwood, I think that you should take Mack with you when you go over to East Boston to ask questions."

Peter looked at Fanny. She nodded. He needed to do whatever Jake told him. He sighed and turned to Mack. "Detective McNally, I'd appreciate your assistance in this."

Mack glowed. "You got it."

"I'm afraid I haven't been assigned a car, so we'll have to take the subway over," Peter told him and, with a final nod to Fanny, he left.

36

CHAPTER TEN

Mack grinned. Before he could follow, Jake said to him, "Behave yourself."

Chapter Eleven

Peter Attwood grasped the side door of the old Model T Ford as Mack bounced over the ramp from the ferry to the pavement of East Boston. Dr. Magrath had explained with pride that the rickety vehicle was named Suffolk Sue and he had customized its features himself. The automobile must have been twenty years old but, apparently, it was a trademark of the eccentric medical examiner. Peter's teeth chattered as they rattled over the pavements. The extra lights and bells shook like they would fall off. Peter fervently wished Mack had not managed to convince Dr. Magrath to let them take his motorcar. But it was too late. They'd hurried down to the ferry before he could object. Crossing the inner harbor had frozen his face despite the fluffy scarf. Mack seemed to be enjoying himself as he clanged one of the sirens.

"Wait," Peter yelled. "Shouldn't we go down Border Street?" He pointed to the left where the street dipped down to docks along the harbor. He remembered they had turned there the day before when they went to the crime scene. The gears screeched as Mack kept heading up the hill on the right-hand fork of the road.

"No. This way." As the old automobile struggled up the hill, the houses got bigger and more impressive. Mack swung the motorcar around in a U-turn to stop in front of a huge house with pillared doorways. The three-story house was painted gray with bow windows and elegantly carved decorations. Steps led to a porch with two large doors.

"Here we are," Mack said, as he hopped out of the Model T. "We're on the street above Border. These houses are at the top of the hill above the three-decker and the Callahan and Sumner warehouses. Callahan has the office here. Lives here, too. They can see all the way down to the docks out the rear windows. The old man has the door on the right; young Bill Junior has the left. Home and office both. He's got another office down in the warehouse, too."

Mack waited impatiently as Peter, grateful to escape unscathed, extracted himself from Suffolk Sue. Then he reached over a massive hand and swiped Peter's hand-knitted cap from his head and thrust it at his chest. "What are you, a ten-year-old? Get rid of the mittens, will you?"

Peter stuffed the hat and mittens in his pocket. So much for comfort. He knew Mack was right, though, and he squirmed, thinking that his superior officer and the others in his office undoubtedly saw him as Mack did, a ten-year-old playing at cops and robbers.

Mack banged on the door, and a maid in a starched apron opened it and led them down a corridor to a room that spanned the back of the building. Two large windows looked out on a panorama. The three-decker where Ingrid had died was down the hill on the right. Beyond were the warehouses, Border Street, and the docks and wharves. Now it made sense to Peter that Callahan would have his office up here. He could keep an eye on everything and meet with his clients.

Bookcases lined the walls, and a large table spread with maps stood in the middle of the room. Back between the windows was a massive carved desk with a leather armchair behind it. Brown leather sofas and chairs formed a grouping on the left side of the room. A man of medium height in his thirties, Bill Callahan, wore a pinstriped suit with a silk vest and a jaunty white carnation in his lapel. He greeted them and directed them to the sofas.

Peter hesitated, but he saw Mack had shut his mouth firmly, so the younger man introduced himself. He tripped up trying to describe Mack's role in the investigation, but Callahan interrupted.

"Of course, I know Mack. Sorry to hear about the layoffs," he said to the big man. Mack grimaced and dropped carefully into one of the leather armchairs. "I think the mayor and the commissioner were too quick to condemn you men, but they're being stubborn."

Sensing that Mack didn't want to discuss the strike, Peter told Callahan he was investigating the death of Conor Leary.

"It's a shock to all of us," Callahan said. His brow furrowed with worry. "The men are anxious. We've got some deadlines coming up, but some of them are calling in sick."

"Are they afraid someone will attack them?" Peter asked.

Mack shifted his bulk in his seat. "Tell him about the other accidents," he said to Callahan.

Callahan shook his head. "The past month has been a disaster. We've had two trucks disabled with broken axles. One of our welding machines caught fire, and one of our floating docks was sunk. Now, Conor killed. It's getting worse all the time. I've hired men to keep watch, but our works are spread out." He waved at the windows. "And we have to take equipment to work sites, the wharves, bridges, tunnels we work on. Someone is out to ruin us."

Mack nodded his head in agreement. Perched on the edge of a sofa, Peter had a notebook and pencil in his hand. "You think Conor Leary was killed by someone who has been sabotaging your yards?"

"I don't know why else anyone would attack him like that. Conor has worked for us for a long time. He came from McKay's shipyard with my father when he started the company. He had a drinking problem. He wasn't dependable, but my father wouldn't let him go, so we used him for odd jobs, delivering messages, watching the docks for us. He did look for a fight sometimes when he was in his cups, but he was a lightweight. Anybody could have knocked him over. That's why I'm wondering if maybe he saw something or someone."

Peter wrote himself a note to look into the suspected sabotage. "Were you present when Mrs. Ericksson was found dead?" He needed to follow up on their theory that Leary saw something about the woman's death.

Callahan looked pained. "That was so sad. It was an awful, awful thing."

"You were there?"

"I was in the office down in the warehouse. When it happened, people yelled there was an accident in the yard of the tenement. We all rushed out, but it was too late."

"Conor Leary was there?"

"Yes. I'm not sure why he was there. He was supposed to be across town at a bridge site. He must have come back for something. He was there in the crowd. A couple of Mack's brothers, his sister, workers from our warehouse, and Sumner's across the way were all crowded around her. Until you came with the patrolmen and shooed us all away. It's an awful thing for her husband, Lars. He's one of our workers."

Peter was too dismayed to remember how he had ordered the body removed, and the crowd dispersed so quickly when Ingrid Ericksson's body was found. Even Callahan remembered him for that. He saw Mack look away, avoiding comment. Peter could feel heat rising up his neck. He was embarrassed. How could he have been so stupid?

Before he could ask Callahan more about Leary and whether the dead man might have seen something before Ingrid's death, he saw Callahan look at Mack. The big man's mouth hung open, and he slowly rose from his seat, raising an arm to point.

They followed his finger and looked out the window, where they could see a tall crane down on the docks. It slowly tilted to the right, then fell against a dock. All three rushed to the window and watched as men surrounded the huge mechanical device. They waved and jumped up and down, but there was nothing they could do as it began to slide into the water.

Chapter Twelve

Callahan yelled, "Noooo" and ran for a door. Mack pursued him. Peter followed. They rushed down an outside stairway that zigzagged across the back of the building, then ran down the steep slope. At the bottom, they rushed past the three-decker tenement where Ingrid Ericksson had died and out onto Border Street.

On the other side, they pounded down wooden docks to get to the farthest one, where the metal crane tipped toward the water, hanging over precariously. A big old man with white hair down to his shoulders and a full beard hauled back on a rope that kept the big machine from falling into the water. Two other men tailed the rope. The machine swayed. Mack and Bill Callahan grabbed the rope, too. But five men weren't enough to haul it back. The wooden dock where they stood was tipped toward the water.

"Good God, go help them. Go on, go on." Peter heard behind him. He looked around and saw Ian Stewart from the Sumner Company wave on a dozen workers. Ian's men swarmed the scene and slowly helped to pull the great crane back until it righted onto the floating dock. The white-haired old man waved Peter and Ian over so they could help him pick up a stout beam of wood and wedge it in front of the machine.

That took the pressure off enough so more of the workers could leave the rope and block the machine securely at various places. Peter moved out of the way with Ian Stewart. Both were shaking with relief.

"What happened?" Peter asked. He watched as the men scrambled around. They knew what they were doing, but it was all a mystery to the police detective.

CHAPTER TWELVE

"It's that damned sabotage," Ian Stewart said quietly. Peter thought he didn't want the old man to hear him. "Callahan has got to do something. That could have been a catastrophe. If that crane fell into the water, we'd all of us be out of business. Our docks and barges would be blocked as much as Callahan's." Ian waved his own men back to their jobs on a nearby dock.

Peter looked at Bill Callahan, who was tying off ropes to anchor the equipment. But Ian pointed at the big old man. "That's William, the father. He's the one who founded the company. Bill is his son, and he's got his fingers in every pie in the city. He's a real climber, that one. But it's the old man who knows the business." The short Scotsman shook his head.

Bill Callahan approached his father, yelling. "Where's Ericksson? Those planks were supposed to hold the thing. What did he do?"

Peter saw the tall Swede stand up on the far side of the crane. His face flushed. The two men glared at each other.

The older Callahan bent over to fish something out of the water. He stood tall with a broken piece of thick wood in his hand. He brandished it. "Don't be blaming Lars. Look at this. It's been sawed through. You see that?" He pointed with his big hands. "That's made by a crosscut saw. It's not Lars's work that's the problem. Someone did this on purpose."

"Not again," Bill Callahan groaned. He grabbed the block of wood from his father. "They're trying to ruin us."

At Peter's side, he heard Ian Stewart growl. "They'll ruin all of us with that kind of stunt. And poor Ericksson. He's still grieving his wife and Billy boy is trying to get him fired. Enough."

Ian stalked over to the dock, skirting the Callahans as he went around and took Lars Erickson by the arm. "Come along. You should be home with your daughter. Come on, then." He led the silent man back toward the shore.

Peter looked around for his companion as the Callahans worked with their men to secure the dock area. He saw Mack leaning down toward a small boat full of men who looked very much like Mack himself. Peter wondered if he was guilty of assuming all big Irish working men looked alike, but then he realized Mack must know the men the way he was swearing at them.

"Get out of there, will ya?" Mack yelled. "I'll tell Kate, and you'll be sorry."

"Ah, get away with you," one of the men shouted back. "We're fishing, is all."

"Fishing? You? Fishing for easy money, Sean McNally, if I know you. And what're you doing with that old rascal in the back? You think I don't know about Big Tim and his schemes? You get yourselves mucked up with that old sinner and there'll be hell to pay I promise you."

"Ah, get away with you. Go to one of your meetings, why don't you?" Sean sneered back.

Peter realized this must be one of the five brothers Mack was yelling at. But despite the talkback, the younger brother paddled his overloaded boat away from Mack's yells. Peter watched as the big ex-detective shook himself like a dog and muttered curses under his breath. When he noticed Peter, he trotted over.

"Let's go look for that murder weapon, shall we?"

Chapter Thirteen

Detective Peter Attwood heard Mack, the big Irishman, curse from inside the wooden storage box that leaned against the brick wall of Callahan & Sons. Mack had cheerfully led the way to the place where they'd found Conor Leary's body and in two leaps, he had bounded into the box. Peter could hear him routing around in there.

Taking a big breath, the young detective unwrapped the scarf his sister had knitted for him and removed the matching hat and gloves, carefully laying them down. The task was unappealing, but Dr. Magrath had ordered them to find the weapon used to bash Leary's head. Peter knew it was another mark against him that he had come away without the weapon the day before.

"Looking for something?"

Startled, Peter looked over his shoulder and saw Ian Stewart, manager of the Sumner Company, knocking his pipe against his teeth as he watched.

"We're looking for the weapon used to kill Conor Leary," Peter explained. He glanced over to where Mack was grunting in the storage box. He should have helped, but he saw a chance to use his detective skills to find out more about what was happening here on the East Boston docks. Determined to act like a real detective and happy to leave the search to Mack, he faced Stewart.

"You took Lars Ericksson away from over there." He nodded toward the docks. "What was that argument between him and Mr. Callahan?"

Stewart considered the question while he dug ashes out of his pipe. "Well, now, there's some bad blood between the two men. You see, Lars gets along real well with old man Callahan. They think alike. They're both men that work with their hands. Not a lot of talk from them. They'll play chess for hours at Ericksson's place with barely a word spoken. I've tried to lure Lars away from that company a couple of times. He's a fine master carpenter. But he's loyal to the old man."

"Are you saying the younger Callahan resents Ericksson because of the time he spends with the father?" Peter asked. There had been something bitter in the confrontation, although Peter had thought the rancor came more from the big Swede than from Bill Callahan. Perhaps he'd been wrong.

Stewart concentrated on filling the pipe from a small bag. He glanced at Peter from under wiry eyebrows. "Could be. But also, Lars was a wee bit jealous. He thought there was something going on between Bill Callahan and his wife." Stewart waved the pipe with a large gesture. "It was nonsense, as I kept telling him. All in his head. The man was just courteous to Ingrid, and she was pleasant back. But these gloomy Swedes." He shook his head. "Lugubrious, that's what he is. I try to tell him it's all in his head, but he's got the notion, and it's stuck there."

Peter straightened and crossed his arms over his chest. The wind was cold. His ears began to sting, but he wanted to consider what Stewart was suggesting.

Stewart took his silence as disbelief. "That young Bill Callahan is a bit of a smarmy one. You could see how Lars could get the wrong idea. Bill's always glad-handing a crowd, knowing everybody's name," he scoffed. "He hangs around with politicians, like that Fitzgerald. Picks it up from them. Not like his old man at all. Callahan Senior is a salt of the earth guy."

Peter wondered if Stewart disliked Bill Callahan because he ran a company that competed with his own. He glanced up at the small, carefully labeled sign over the door across the alley. It read "Sumner Co." "Which Sumner owns your company?" It was an old family name familiar to Peter from the Back Bay and North Shore.

Stewart grinned. "That would be Augustus Lane Sumner, descendant of the Sumner who originally built on this peninsula."

"Ah, I think I've met him. He has a boat up in Marblehead. Races at the club where my father is a member." Peter had grown up crewing for his father in sailboat races at the yacht club there. Memories stung him, so he almost flinched. He tried not to show his distaste. His father was a tyrant at the helm, dressing down any crew member who flubbed a tack. He'd vowed to himself that this past summer would be the last time he crewed for his father. Not that he'd wanted him after Peter joined the force. Rupert Attwood III looked down his long nose at his second son's occupation. Peter tried not to hold it against Augustus Sumner, that he was part of the Marblehead crowd.

"Aye, that's his passion," Stewart was saying. "Unlike the Callahans, he's not likely to be found at the docks here, only those up in Marblehead where he keeps his yacht."

"Must give you a free hand to run the place as you like." Peter wondered if Bill Callahan suffered by having his father hanging over his shoulder all the time. He thought the Scotsman's gossip about Bill Callahan might come from a business rivalry. The man seemed good-natured about it, though.

"Yes, I get to make a lot of the decisions, but I get all the blame, too." He pointed at the Callahan building. "Still, I do wish Mr. Sumner might be a bit chummier with the local pols. They divvy out the contracts for the city and, despite our man's family name and long history with the place, that Bill Callahan is stealing contracts out from under Mr. Sumner's nose lately." He shook his head.

A loud yell came from the storage bin, and Mack's big body bounced up to the rim, then down in two steps. He brandished a three-foot-long piece of metal. "Here it is!"

Chapter Fourteen

Fanny stopped at the door of the morgue and took a breath. She moved the carpet bag to her left hand as she rang the bell. She wasn't at all sure how Jake would react to her latest idea.

Edwin answered the bell and ushered her into Jake's crowded office. Jake was filling out forms, and he ignored her until he was finished. Blotting the form and then capping the ink bottle, he sat back.

"To what do I owe this visit?" He frowned, eyeing the heavy bag she'd dropped at her feet. "Not planning on knitting, are you?" There were a couple of needles sticking out.

Fanny huffed. He was in a mood. Gruff was his normal attitude, though, so she didn't take it personally. "No, it's for the case."

"Case?" He raised an eyebrow. "What case?"

"The death of that poor woman in East Boston," Fanny said. He was teasing her. He got her goat every time. She reached down to pull a doll out of the bag.

"What's this all about?" Jake demanded.

"The angle of the shot. During the autopsy, you mentioned the angle of the shot that killed Ingrid Ericsson was a puzzle. So, let's solve it." Pulling one of the knitting needles from the bag, she handed doll and needle across the desk. "Show me."

"Oh, I see." He examined the rag doll. It had a round face with yarn for hair and wore a checkered skirt. He twirled the needle.

He was wasting time. "It's all right," Fanny told him. "It's just an old doll Cornelia had. You can pierce it with the needle. Show me how Ingrid

Ericksson was shot by using the needle."

"Hmmm." Jake turned the doll over and examined the back. He carefully forced the needle in just at the waist, moved it around a bit, then let it exit from the breast.

"So, the shot was at an upward trajectory," she said. "From somewhere below."

He shook his head. "Or down. Or from behind." He stood the doll up and bent her in half at the waist. "She was hanging clothes, remember. She could have bent down to get at the clothes in the basket."

"Could her husband have come out with his rifle and shot her?"

Jake sat back, crossing his arms as Fanny manipulated the doll. She could see that she'd got him thinking. "There were no powder burns on the wound. I'd expect burns if he was that close."

"What if he was below? He said he was in their apartment, but he could have lied." Fanny reached down and pulled her sketchbook from the bag. Paging through, she found the sketch of the three-decker and surrounding buildings. On the top floor where the Erickssons lived, laundry hung from lines strung from one side of the porch to the other. A chair was set beneath, by the railing, to allow Ingrid to step up to reach the laundry. "Do you think the shot could have come from the roof of the Callahan warehouse? Or from the ground?"

Jake moved the doll to the side with a grunt. "The angle of the shot is odd, but it can be explained by a number of different possibilities and even some we may not have thought of. You'd be surprised how many ways stupidly weird circumstances can lead to unfounded conclusions."

Fanny picked up the doll, with the knitting needle slanting through its torso. She had hoped her idea about the angle of the shot would be conclusive.

"It's still something that will have to be explained in the long run," Jake told her. "It's a very curious thing. When we do know what happened, it would be instructive to have a demonstration. Perhaps a cast." He reached across and took the doll, turning it in his hand. "We use casts sometimes in teaching medical students."

"Paper mâché," Fanny said. "We could make a cast. And we could do the same for other wounds. It could be used to teach how to look at such things." In a flash, she had a picture in her mind of a bookcase full of casts of gunshot wounds.

"Yes," Jake ruminated. "Hmm. That could be helpful. There are some other cases I can recall where a cast of the wound could be instructive. Cases where the first assumption turned out to be totally wrong."

Fanny smiled. This was exactly what she wanted. She knew she could be helpful.

Jake shook his head. "Investigators are not exactly lined up waiting to be taught about this kind of thing, you know. They're mostly pretty stubborn men with their own opinions about anything."

But Fanny knew Peter Attwood would be a willing student. She thought that she and Jake together could instruct a new kind of detective. Jake might be right about stubborn, hard men, but if a new kind of investigator could get results, that had to mean something to the higher-ups. She was sure of it. How to convince Jake? "Surely, if we can explain a complicated case like the death of Ingrid Ericksson, the authorities will recognize the need for better training of their detectives."

Jake handed her the doll. "You've no idea. Commissioner Curtis has no interest in training detectives in the niceties of investigation. He's intent on purging the police of the men who dared to strike." He shook his head. "We've still got militia men guarding some of the streets. The sorry thing is if O'Meara were still Commissioner, none of this would have happened and you could have thought of better training programs. Right now, it's the old Yankees trying to reassert control of the city streets. Public safety is where they put their efforts, not murder investigations."

Fanny raised her head from the bag where she was stowing her little doll. "But surely—" she began.

"No, Fanny, you don't understand. Stephen O'Meara was an unusual man. He was Irish Catholic, but he was a Republican."

"Republican? I thought all the Boston Irish were Democrats?"

"That's one of the things that made him unusual." Jake stood and began to pace in his crowded office. "O'Meara managed to steer the police department between the Irish mayors, like Fitzgerald and Curley, and the Yankee governors in the State House."

Fanny frowned. "I thought the Republicans were worried about so many Irish on the police force. I would think they'd support the police as their voters."

"You'd think that, but the state has appointed the police commissioner since back in the eighties. Fitz and Curley didn't give a fig about the police because they couldn't appoint any of their followers to jobs. O'Meara was appointed by a Republican governor, but he prided himself on keeping the jobs nonpolitical."

Fanny was puzzled.

Jake stopped in front of her. "It's all about the money. The state held all the appointment power, but the department had to be funded by the city. It was an impossible situation, but somehow, O'Meara handled it without losing the respect of his men. It was the mayors who refused to give him the money to meet the demands of the men."

Fanny could see that Jake regretted the death of the previous police commissioner. She wondered if O'Meara had been a personal friend.

Jake returned to his seat behind the desk and pounded his fist. "This Curtis is a nasty old pol who wants revenge on men who defied him by forming a union, and he's got the governor behind him. He's bound and determined to fill the positions quickly and blacklist the strikers. He's not going to expend time, effort, or money on training them. He just wants bodies."

Fanny felt defeated by Jake's outburst. Men and their politics. The police were responsible for keeping the city streets clear of rioters like the ones who had taken advantage of the police strike. But they were also responsible for finding those guilty of murder. The murders of Ingrid Ericksson and Conor Leary must be solved, and Fanny held on to her belief that methods used to solve such a complicated case would be recognized and then, the need to improve the training of police would be a logical conclusion. Edwin was finding out about various new techniques to identify criminals and bring them to justice. Surely, Boston needed to keep up with the rest of the world. Jake was pessimistic about change in police procedures, but Fanny was determined to find a way to prove him wrong.

Chapter Fifteen

Peter trudged toward the three-decker. Ingrid Ericksson had fallen to her death from the balcony. Where was Mack? When they returned to the Callahan warehouse, the ex-detective had been helpful in finding the men who worked with Leary and getting them to talk. But, halfway through the interviews, Mack had lost interest and wandered away. Peter thought the Irishman might have spotted two of his brothers walking by and left to speak to them. It irked him that Mack just walked away with no excuse. Then he remembered the Irishman wasn't being paid for his time, as Peter was, so he returned to the interviews by himself. He hated to admit that he wanted the experienced detective's oversight, but he did. Mack was blunt with his interruptions in the early interviews, but Peter recognized that he learned from Mack's questions.

On his own, Peter talked to half a dozen men who were shocked by Conor Leary's death. They happily talked about how Leary drank on the job, but he'd been an employee so long his lapses were overlooked by management. Leary was around when old man Callahan started the company. A few years back, Leary lost his wife and kids when drink got the best of him. Even then, the Callahans kept him on. When it came to the brutal beating that caused Leary's death, the men's mouths closed. Even Mack hadn't been able to get a comment in the earlier interviews. Peter noticed the ex-detective's eyes narrowed at the stubborn wall of silence, and he wondered if Mack knew what they were hiding.

When the last man clammed up about the beating, Peter shut his notebook and decided to find Mack and head back to the morgue to report to Dr.

Magrath. Perhaps he should report to his own superior at the police station, but Peter wanted to hear what Mack and the medical examiner had to say first. He hoped Mrs. Lee's suggestion that Dr. Magrath could help him solve the case was true. He felt a deep hole in his confidence and was grasping at anything to pull himself up. He had no desire to face the Chief Detective without running his work by Magrath, and even Mack, before that confrontation. He desperately wanted to avoid his father's scoffing if he lost his new job.

He headed over to the three-decker, where he found the back door open. He stepped inside. Mack must be in the first-floor apartment he shared with his brothers. He was about to knock and call out, but he remembered Kate Gallagher just in time. She wouldn't thank him if he woke sleeping children, and he didn't relish a tongue lashing from the hearty young woman. The walls of the rickety tenement were thin.

Before stepping to the door for a quiet knock, he heard voices. They were from the Ericksson apartment on the third floor.

"Now, Lars. It's very important that you stop making these accusations. You know they're not true. It's a terrible thing that happened to Ingrid, but you mustn't let grief drive you to distraction. Think of your daughter. She needs you." It was a woman's voice.

Peter took the steps two at a time to reach the third floor. The door was open, and a woman in her thirties was looming over Lars Ericksson, who sat before her on a couch with his head hung low. The woman reminded him of his brother's wife or his grandmother's younger women friends. Yet, with a difference. She wore a fashionably tall hat with a black feather and a dark woolen suit with a lace-trimmed blouse, styles like the women in his family wore. Peter wondered if she wore the outfit for the very first time, it was so sleek and perfect. He thought he could place her as a type, but then she seemed a little off-key. It was all a bit too new, bright, and shiny.

Hearing him, the woman turned toward the doorway. "Yes. Are you looking for someone?" she asked. She was imperious.

Peter stood up straight. "I'm Detective Attwood," he opened his overcoat to display his gold badge. "I have a few questions for Mr. Ericksson."

For a moment, her eyes glazed over, then she took a step toward him, holding out a gloved hand. "How do you do? I'm Mrs. William H. Callahan Jr. I was just talking to Mr. Ericksson." She considered him. "You were on the docks when that accident happened, weren't you? I watched from our back windows. I saw Mr. Ericksson having words with my husband, and I wanted to be sure things were, ah, settled between them."

Peter didn't know what to say. Ian Stewart had told him that Ericksson was jealous of Bill Callahan. Here was Callahan's wife inserting herself into the situation. It was awkward.

She pursed her lips. "I see you overheard. Lars here had the mistaken impression there was something between his wife Ingrid and my husband. He can't seem to talk to Bill about it without coming to blows. I wanted to let him know he is completely mistaken. There was no romantic attachment between poor Ingrid and my husband. Someone's been putting ideas in his head, and I want to make him understand it's a lie, plain and simple."

She was certainly a force to be contended with. Peter could see that. She reminded him of some of his grandmother's suffragist friends. Vehement. Like most men, Lars was cowed by so much feminine aggression. Peter sympathized. He cleared his throat.

"I see. Did you know Mrs. Ericksson well?"

"She did some mending for me from time to time. And we all know Lars as he's a great friend of my father-in-law. They play chess. My father-in-law and my husband both have a lot of respect for Mr. Ericksson's skills as a carpenter. He's very important to the company."

"Do you have any idea who would want to hurt Mrs. Ericksson?"

"Goodness, no. She was a lovely young woman and mother." Mrs. Callahan shook her head. "It's such a tragedy. It's no wonder poor Lars, here, is off his head. There's no reason in the world for anyone to hurt Ingrid."

"You're aware that a Mr. Conor Leary was also found dead? Are you acquainted with him?"

"Not really." She looked like she wanted to sniff in distaste but refrained with an effort. "I believe he had a drinking problem. Mr. Callahan senior is very loyal to men who've been with him from when he started the company.

55

Conor Leary was certainly someone who could have made enemies among the ruffians down at the docks."

"Any particular ruffians? Do you know of some?" Peter asked. He could use a lead from anyone. While Mrs. Callahan didn't seem like someone who'd spend time with "ruffians," he knew not to underestimate the resources of competent women. His grandmother had taught him that.

At that moment, Mack came pounding up the stairs carrying an iron bar wrapped in brown paper. It was the weapon he'd found in the storage bin, that they believed killed Conor Leary. They needed to get it back to Dr. Magrath at the morgue. Mack pushed Peter aside to step into the room. "What's going on? I could hear you all from downstairs. You'd better hush it up, or Kate will skin you. Oh, it's you, Eileen. What're you up to? Getting a scoop for your rag?" He turned to Peter. "Have you met our lady reporter? This is Bill's wife, Eileen Callahan. She's a cut above the likes of us, but she puts out a weekly sheet Bill's dad bought for her. *East Boston News.*"

Mrs. Callahan was unruffled by Mack. "This has nothing to do with the paper. I was just talking to Lars. He's been imagining that there was something between Bill and Ingrid, and I just wanted to set him straight. To reassure him that nothing like that was going on."

"Oh, *that,*" Mack exclaimed. He bent toward the Swede on the couch. "Lars, man, you know there's nothing to that. Nothing at all. You're out of your head with grief. We all know it, and we don't blame you. But, don't be getting stupid ideas. Ingrid was a good girl. She was all yours. Always yours."

Lars Ericksson's bowed head hadn't moved. Peter couldn't tell if he was even listening.

"For the love of…" Mack huffed. He turned to Mrs. Callahan. "Look, I'll get Kate to look after him. She's got the babe already."

"Yes. That's a good idea," she said. "Goodbye, Lars. Just know we're all here to help you, so if you need anything, you tell Mack here, or Mrs. Gallagher, and we'll get you what you want. Don't worry about the funeral. Bill and I and, of course, Bill's dad will cover the cost. You're not to brood about that. And do think about little Lilly." She turned to go, nodding to Peter as she left.

Mack stood looking down at Lars. "You're just a fine old mess, man, aren't you? Can't blame you when you lost a grand woman like that, but you've got to pull yourself together."

Chapter Sixteen

Jake finished an autopsy in the operation theater and left Edwin to oversee the cleanup by the Harvard medical students. They were a mixed lot. Some were ardent students; they'd probably go into research or become arrogant surgeons. Most were relaxed, content to learn enough to fulfill their parents' ambitions. Quite a few had physician fathers or uncles and lived in the certainty that they'd take over a practice all in good time. Jake found them too complacent for the most part. He preferred working with Edwin and Peter, young men who were excited by what they were struggling to discover in the murder case.

So, he was glad when he saw Mack march in, followed by a more reluctant young Peter. Jake was looking forward to quizzing them on the puzzle of the deaths in East Boston. He suspected young Peter's job would be on the line with superiors who didn't welcome a Brahmin into their ranks. From Jake's point of view, that was a good thing. He'd be hungry to find the facts. And good old Mack would pride himself on beating the younger man to the punch. Sure enough, the big man followed Jake into his office, waving a paper-wrapped object that he placed on the desk as Jake sat down.

"What's this?"

"The murder weapon! As requested," Mack grinned.

Peter followed him in. "Mack found it in the storage bin."

Jake could tell the young detective was feeling sheepish about not having found it during the first visit. But Mack had missed it, too. At least they'd found it when they returned to East Boston. "Let this be a lesson to you. The weapon should have been found when we found the body. Even before the autopsy, it was clear that Leary was beaten to death. Not shot." He pointed to the package on the table in front of him. "You've got to be more careful at a crime scene." He saw Peter cringe, no doubt remembering they'd found Leary's body when they had to return to the scene because they'd taken Ingrid's body away before they realized she was shot. Once again, they'd been too quick to remove Leary's body without the murder weapon. "You should know better, Mack," he scolded the ex-detective, who was looking smug.

"Let me take a look." Jake unwrapped the paper to find a thick piece of metal broken off from something. Jake examined the jagged end. "There's blood and hair here. Where did it come from? Could you tell?"

Mack jumped in before Peter could speak. "It's a piece from that stack of steel in the corner there. It's all part of a short railway bridge the Callahan's pulled down. They kept it to be reused. Steel's expensive these days, and they can always find a use for it."

"And what can we make of that?" Jake challenged the two men. Mack was still standing, looming over the desk. Peter had collapsed on the visitor's chair. He looked discouraged. "What do you say, Detective Attwood?" Jake put up a hand to stop Mack from speaking. The big man rolled his eyes and leaned back against a wooden filing cabinet, crossing his arms over his chest.

Peter looked up. Jake suspected he was a good student at Harvard. Answering test questions had been drilled into him. He frowned. "Well, I suppose it means whoever beat Leary didn't bring a weapon with him; he picked it up off the ground."

"And that tells you..." Jake prompted.

"Ah, he hadn't planned to kill the man. Perhaps they argued, and the killer lost his temper with Leary."

"Possibly. Or he hadn't expected to see him there and took advantage of the opportunity. Perhaps he would have planned more carefully, but for some reason, he couldn't wait and had to act quickly."

Jake still held a hand up to silence Mack, who was bursting to get his opinion into the discussion. Jake wanted to hear what the young detective had to say.

"Leary must have been a serious threat. He must have known something or threatened the person. Could he have seen who shot Ingrid Ericksson?"

Mack sank back against the cabinet like a balloon that had deflated. Jake assumed the big Irishman had been about to suggest the same thing.

"It's certainly a possibility. What did you learn from his coworkers?"

Peter sighed. "Not much. They didn't particularly like the fellow. He was drunk a lot. I think some of them resented that the Callahans let him get away with so much but kept paying him. Not enough to want to beat him to death, though. But something else happened while we were there."

He told Jake about the near accident on the harbor-wharf and the heated argument between Bill Callahan and Lars Ericksson.

"He's mad with grief, that one," Mack said. "You can't take notice of what he says."

Jake was interested in the accident. "So, this is not the first time something like that has happened? Do they suspect sabotage?"

"It's been going on for the past month from what the men said," Peter told him. "The crane that almost fell had been blocked in place by Lars."

"It was sabotage," Mack protested. "Old Will, Bill's father, found the block of wood half sawed through. It was bound to give. Lars wouldn't do a thing like that. He's friends with the old man, and it's his livelihood besides."

"Ian Stewart from the Sumner company said he's tried to lure Ericksson away to his company, but the Swede's too loyal to the Callahans," Peter told them.

Jake considered the information. "So, who killed Mrs. Ericksson? And who killed Leary?"

Peter shrugged. "I met Bill Callahan's wife. She was scolding Ericksson. She doesn't believe her husband was involved with Ingrid."

"Of course, he wasn't," Mack nearly shouted. "That's the dumbest thing anybody said. Ingrid was devoted to her husband and little Lilly. It's a bad thing when the poor woman's not alive to defend herself, and they're sullying her name. It's an awful thing."

Jake wondered why Mack was so defensive of Bill Callahan. Did he owe him something? Peter seemed more objective on the subject of the possible wayward tendencies of the dead woman. The young detective would have to report back to his superiors. And soon. "What will you tell them back at the station?"

Peter stood up. "That we found the murder weapon. I guess I'll describe the near accident at the dock. Mention the sabotage. Maybe Leary was killed because he knew something about that. Maybe Mrs. Ericksson saw something. They've got a view of the factory yard from the house." He shrugged. "I'll need to tell them about the argument between Bill Callahan and Lars Ericksson." He saw Mack's deep frown. "I can't leave that out. I'll say how Ericksson seems to be out of his mind with grief, of course."

"Don't be trying to pin this on Callahan," Mack insisted.

Jake intervened. "Well, if even his wife is anxious to put down rumors about the dead woman and her husband, you've got to question whether there was something there. Who's your superior, Detective Attwood?"

Peter gritted his teeth. "Chief Detective McKenna."

"God help ya," said Mack.

Chapter Seventeen

Peter straightened his spine and entered the station house. He climbed worn stairs to the detectives' large open room on the second floor. The air was thick with cigar smoke rising to electric lights that hung down from the ceiling. Eight scarred wooden desks were piled with newspapers, typed reports, and dirty mugs. Only two desks were occupied, and the shirt-sleeved men quickly banged desk drawers shut at the sight of Peter. He guessed they'd had a card game going. They practically growled when they recognized him and sat back in their swivel chairs.

He nodded, but the only response was cold glares. He sighed. The rest of the detectives were probably out on the streets. It was a perk of the job that they could come and go as they pleased. Some of them would be having an evening whiskey at a bar with the excuse that they were gathering intelligence. As far as he knew, he was the only one who had to report to the chief detective every evening.

Chief Detective McKenna had a private office with a door. Peter knew to knock before entering. It gave McKenna time to move a bottle and glass to a deep drawer. Peter had recognized the chief's contempt for him and assumed it was because he'd been promoted without experience. He'd hoped the rough treatment he'd gotten so far was normal training for a new man on the team. But the reaction he'd gotten from Mack and Dr. Magrath when they heard McKenna's name shook that belief. Mack had nothing but swear words to describe the chief detective, and Magrath had looked wary and advised him to be careful. The medical examiner had exchanged a look with his assistant Edwin. That young man had seemed to pity Peter when he let him out the morgue door, wishing him luck. Peter's heart sank.

And here he was, face to face with the man. McKenna was fleshy, broad-shouldered, and had a pot belly. He had a brown mustache, thick eyebrows, and a nose that was red and veined. A mop of brown hair was threaded with some silver. His omnipresent bowler hat sat on the corner of his desk, ready to be jammed on his head as soon as he rose. Peter had overheard a comment that seemed to indicate the chief detective kept rooms in a local brothel, but he couldn't believe it. Perhaps he'd ask Dr. Magrath. It couldn't be true.

"You," McKenna sneered. "Find any more accident victims who were shot in the back? You know that makes us look like fools, don't you? If you want to keep on here, you'd better clean this up fast. Who shot the woman? And I heard there's another corpse, too." He picked up a form from his desk. "That old son of a bitch Magrath says he was beaten to death. Did you find who did that?"

Peter gave a succinct report on what they had seen and done in East Boston. He almost mentioned Mack, but based on the curse-ridden description the ex-detective had given about the chief detective, he decided to leave the big Irishman out. After the report, Peter remained standing in front of the glowering man like a schoolboy in the principal's office. He knew Chief Sullivan, who had originally recruited him, would never treat him like this. He feared McKenna was itching to get rid of him, and he'd use any blunders on his first murder case to do it, but Peter had a stubborn streak he got from his grandmother, so he stood his ground.

"So, what're you waiting for? This Bill Callahan must have shot the woman. He was having a fling with her; he didn't want his missus to find out, so he got rid of her. What more do you need? Most likely, that old drunk saw something, tried to blackmail Callahan, and got hit over the head for his troubles."

"But we've no evidence that Callahan did anything." Peter couldn't go along with this. He knew McKenna would hate him for daring to disagree, but he couldn't jump to such a conclusion. "We don't know if Callahan even owns a gun, and we found the weapon that was used on Leary. It was an iron bar from the scrap pile on the corner. Anyone could have picked it up."

McKenna waved a hand as if waving away the evidence. Could he really ignore the questions?

"We can't just arrest Callahan. We have a gun that belongs to Lars Ericksson, the husband. He could have killed her. Besides, most people have assured us that the dead woman had no relationship to Mr. Callahan."

"'Us?' You and who else?"

Peter's nerves tingled with a warning of danger. Mentioning Mack was not something he should do. "Dr. Magrath. We discussed it when I brought him the iron bar that we-I-found in the storage bin where we found Leary. He also has Ericksson's gun to examine." Peter noticed a reaction from McKenna at the name of the medical examiner. He sensed that McKenna was wary of the well-known official. "I don't think Dr. Magrath would be satisfied if we charged Mr. Callahan without sufficient evidence."

McKenna jumped up from behind the desk and confronted Peter, breathing whiskey fumes into his face. "That old lush. Him and that biddy from Beacon Hill. I know them. I won't have them interfering with our investigations. You got that?" He poked a finger into Peter's breast. "I know this Callahan. He's one to kiss the asses of these old Brahmins. Wants to be one of them. He's got some of those Democratic politicians in his pocket. Giving them money for their campaigns." His eyes narrowed, and he looked slyly at Peter, who was holding his breath against the fumes. "Magrath is one of them old Yankees himself. The kind Callahan and his ilk like to imitate. I'll bet he likes you, doesn't he, boy? Gonna take you under his wing, I'll bet. Heh, heh, we'll see about that." He stepped back from Peter who let his breath out with a sigh of relief as McKenna headed back behind his desk and took out a bottle and glass from the deep drawer.

"Well, we wouldn't want our dear old Dr. Magrath to be unhappy with our investigation, now, would we? Tell you what, 'Detective,' you go back to that old man Magrath and see how he helps you. I'll be waiting right here for that arrest. I'll give it a couple more days and if you haven't got your man, I'll just have to give you some help of my own. Show you how it's done, see?" He filled the glass and toasted it to Peter. "Now, get out of my office, you sniveling toad."

Peter stared. A couple of days? That was the end of the week. Was McKenna really threatening to arrest Bill Callahan himself if Peter didn't arrest him by Friday? Gulping, the young detective rushed out of the room. He didn't believe it. Even McKenna couldn't just throw a local businessman in jail because he didn't like him. Could he?

Chapter Eighteen

"Sean!" Mack yelled. He heard a baby cry and cringed. Kate would kill him for waking the kid. He stepped inside the first-floor apartment and shut the door gently, hoping to avoid his sister. He could hear a muffled curse from above.

There was no one in the small parlor of the bachelor apartment. Clothes were dropped on chairs and the floor. Empty bottles stood on the low table. No one in the bedroom shared by three of his brothers. Another mess in there. Kate came in once a week and shouted at them while she got them to pick up their dirty laundry and take it to a tub in the basement. Looked like it was about time.

The bathroom door was shut, so Mack pounded on it. "Sean," he whispered hoarsely.

The door opened. It was Alfie, getting ready for his night watchman job. "He's out. What in the name of God is your problem, man? You know Kate will fry you if you wake the babes."

Mack had already done that. "Never mind that. Where is that son of a b? I want to talk to him. He's hanging around with old Tim, and he knows what a nasty lad that one is. What's he thinking?"

Alfie turned back to the cracked mirror to wipe off bits of soap. His shoulders hunched.

"Where is he?" Mack demanded.

"Ask Kate."

"What do you mean, ask Kate? Why Kate? Where..." Alfie slammed the door in his face. Mack didn't relish facing his younger sister after waking one of her kiddies. But he was a man, wasn't he? He wasn't going to be cowed by a woman, not even Kate.

He straightened up and marched upstairs, knocking gently on the second-floor door when he got there.

Kate swung it open, a child on her shoulder. She frowned at him. "It's yourself making all that noise? How many times have I told you to shut up when it's evening like this? I just get them down, and one of you louts bangs around like an earthquake. Here, come in and shut that door, would you."

Mack followed her into her small kitchen at the back of the apartment. The child was burbling happily, and the others were soundless, so he could see she wasn't too upset. A good thing.

"Where's Sean? And why is Alfie telling me to ask you about it? Do you know what Sean's been up to? I want a word with him."

Kate stopped juggling the baby in her arms and put her down in a cradle she kept in the kitchen. Looking at her back, Mack sensed there was something wrong. "The pot's still hot. Let me give you a mug of tea." She moved away to the stove.

Mack could feel his face tingle with a rush of blood. What was going on here? "I don't want tea, woman. I want information. Where is he?"

She ignored him and filled two mugs with tea, spilling some milk and spooning some sugar before she brought them over. "That's new milk, that is. Joe brought it home. He's abed already; he had a hard shift."

Mack ignored the mug she put before him as she sat opposite. What was she going on about? He had nothing against her milquetoast fireman husband. He was looking for Sean. "What in the name of all that's holy are you and Alfie on about? I saw Sean with that old sinner Tim today. You know he's bad news. I need to set him straight about that old monster. So, tell me, *where is Sean?*"

She wouldn't look at him. "Ah, Mack, I'm sorry, luv. He's out with Mary Delaney. I'm thinking Alfie didn't want to be the one to tell you, dear."

Mack felt like an arrow had pierced him in the chest. Mary Delaney and Sean. The traitor. His own brother. Mack clutched his hands in fists and felt the blood boiling in his veins.

"I suppose Alfie was afraid you'd be mad, and you might punch him with Sean not being around to receive your wrath. But he knew you wouldn't be raising your voice or your hand to me, now, would you?" She stared at him until he calmed down and unclenched his hands.

"Now, you listen, Mack. We all know you and Mary were walking out. And we all know she stopped walking out with you during the strike."

"She wanted me to take a watchman job like Alfie. I'm not so desperate as that. I'm a police officer, not a damned nightwatchman." And he wasn't going to let some woman tell him what to do, not even Mary.

"Yes, well, she wanted to marry and have kiddies, and with you refusing to take a job…"

"I have a job. Those bastards are trying to take it away from me. A man has to fight. You can't just stand there and let them win. You have to stand up to them."

"Mack, listen to me. They've got state militia brought in to quell the riots. They've blacklisted you and the rest of them. Now, they've given your jobs away to other men. I know you don't want to face it. You just meet and meet and drink and drink. What do you expect a young woman like Mary to do then? What's done is done. If you want to hang on to a lost cause, that's your choice, but you cannot expect her to do it."

Mack felt dizzy with suppressed rage, but he looked across at his sister and saw only pity and kindness in her gaze. He couldn't stand it. She felt sorry for him. He stood up to release some of the pent-up energy and started pacing to the sink and back.

"So, she's out with Sean? Sean? How could she? How could *he*? Me own brother for crying out loud."

Kate sighed. "That's not fair, and you know it. Mary was going with Sean before you. You were the one lured her away from your little brother."

Mack flinched. Like salt rubbed into a wound, that was. His own family were all against him. His stomach felt like he'd swallowed a stone. Sean.

"Sean's employed, is he? Then what's he doing in a boat with Big Tim? That scheming blind old bugger?"

Kate looked surprised. "I don't know, I'm sure. Sean's working for Liam

Kelly at the Black Rose. Perhaps he was doing something for him."

"And how long is the Black Rose going to run with prohibition coming, eh? He's working in a pub that'll have no liquor come the new year. And having a hard time getting anything worth drinking even before that." Prohibition was a sword hanging over every publican's head as it was due to go into force in January. During the war, the government had limited alcohol consumption by keeping grain for wartime productions, but the bar owners in Boston had found ways around that. Come the new year, there'd be no more getting around it. Mack and his family and friends knew that prohibition was aimed at working men like them. It was another case of the Brahmin Yankees wanting to put down the newcomer immigrants. But the dries had won out against the wets, and the law would go into effect. Mack didn't envy the men who'd have to enforce it. For the life of him, he didn't see how it would work. Sean's employer would be out of business. How could Mary not see that?

Kate scoffed. "You know Liam will find a way—sell food or whatever. The thing is, Sean is employed, and you're not."

"Sean is dallying with Big Tim. It's okay to make your money with that scoundrel, is it? You know he's been feuding with that Gustin Gang in South Boston. No telling what mischief he'll be getting the boys into now."

"Now, don't you go accusing your own brother of doing something illegal. You just want a way to say police is the only job worth your trying. It's not. You leave Sean alone. Don't you dare beat your brother up over some girl who doesn't want you. That's not Sean's fault, is what I'm telling you. It's yours."

Mack could feel a wave building. Only Kate could talk to him like that, and his brothers knew it. He wanted to lash out, but he'd never hit a woman. It wasn't in him. Instead, he jumped up and rushed from the room, slamming the front door behind him, hoping he'd woken up all the kids for her. She deserved it, even if he knew she really loved him and wanted to set him straight. He'd set himself straight. To hell with all of them.

Chapter Nineteen

"Faneuil Hall was originally the town hall when Boston was still just a town," Cornelia told Fanny. They stood in the Great Hall of the historic building. Cornelia's grandson was being inducted into the Ancient and Honorable Artillery Company, and Fanny's friend had recruited her to attend. "Now it's used for all sorts of meetings, protests, banquets. The Ancients have had the top two floors for years. They weren't happy to be put out by the State Guard that marched in to help with the police strike riots. The Guard have been using the building as a barracks."

Fanny looked around. The Great Hall was a handsome room with white pillars holding up a second-floor balcony and a high stage at the front under a huge oil painting depicting Daniel Webster giving a speech. It did seem a formal room, perhaps too formal to be used as a "barracks." She thought of the young soldiers she'd helped to find their homes after the great war. They'd certainly be out of place here.

"Poor Peter," Cornelia said. "He'll have a hard time, I'm afraid. It's his older brother, Rupert Attwood IV, who's been accepted. My son-in-law is proud of his first son, who followed him into banking. He has nothing good to say about poor Peter."

A uniformed usher came and asked the spectators to retreat to the sidelines, shooing them like geese. Cornelia led Fanny to a staircase that took them to the balcony. They watched as a troop of men marched into the Great Hall. They were nothing like the displaced young men she remembered from the war. These were older men who wore dark uniforms with bright golden epaulets and braiding. There were no guns, but some of them wore thin rapiers hanging from their yellow belts. When they'd all funneled through the double doors, they stood at attention in ranks.

On the stage, there was a ceremony, inducting seven men into the company and then introducing a few dozen young men. Sons or grandsons of Ancients members who had recently returned from the war in Europe. Those young men reminded Fanny of the men she'd hosted in the home for returning soldiers that had originally brought her to Boston. Dressed in various battle dress, depending on the service they belonged to, they looked comparatively ragtag beside the Ancients.

Cornelia explained to Fanny that the organization was more ceremonial and social than military. It was the oldest chartered military organization, having been established in the 1600s. Members wore uniforms and participated in drills, but they mostly provided pageantry in parades and at other public events. Membership was considered a mark of patriotism, and, of course, limiting membership made it more desirable to be selected.

Men. How odd that they would scramble to be accepted into this ceremonial army that imitated eighteenth-century military traditions when so many young men were anxious to leave behind their memories of military service in the dirty trenches of the recent war in Europe. This was more like playing toy soldiers on a tabletop battlefield. Yet it drew the most influential men in the city.

Peter joined his grandmother and Fanny at the end of the ceremony, and all three went downstairs to congratulate Peter's brother.

"Good for you." Peter shook his brother's hand vigorously.

Rupert was tall and dark-haired like his brother. But he was thicker-waisted and wore a handlebar mustache. He clapped Peter on the shoulder. "Hey, you can do it, too. If you'd just get over playing cops and robbers."

Peter flushed. Fanny thought he looked upset. She doubted it was about his brother's induction into the patriotic organization. It must have to do with the case. She would have liked to ask him how his investigation was going, but a tall man with graying hair, also in uniform, joined them, and she felt a chill in the air. This must be the father, Rupert Attwood III. He stood ramrod straight with his hat tucked under one arm and a tall young woman

71

clutching his other elbow.

Cornelia introduced them. "Mrs. Lee, this is my granddaughter, Holly Attwood, and my son-in-law Rupert." Rupert III bowed slightly. Fanny knew that Cornelia's daughter had died young. She sensed that her friend was none too happy with her son-in-law, but she kept up relations for the sake of her grandchildren.

"Nice to meet you, Mrs. Lee. I hope you've met my son, Rupert, here. We're very proud of him. This is his evening to shine." Rupert III was looking at Peter as he said this. When he let up his glance, his eyes wandered to the crowd behind them. "If you'll excuse me, Cornelia, I need to speak with someone."

Peter's father marched off to speak to another Ancient in a similar uniform with a particularly bright gold braid hanging from his shoulder. Peter's older brother yelled a greeting to another of the inductees and excused himself to his grandmother to pursue a group of young men who were leaving. Fanny resented Rupert's comment about how Peter was merely playing at cops and robbers when she could see that the men of this organization he was so proud to join were less than realistic in their military actions. "Playing," indeed.

She turned to Holly Attwood, who smiled warmly at her. "How do you do, Mrs. Lee. I'm so glad to meet you. I've heard all about you." She was tall for a woman, and thin. Her dark hair was cut in a "bob," and her dark eyes were merry. Fanny liked her immediately. Cornelia had told her that her granddaughter was the image of her dead mother.

"I hope it was good things," Fanny replied.

"Of course." She grabbed her brother Peter's arm. "Peter told me you work with the medical examiner who's going to help him be a great detective. Isn't that so, Peter?"

The young man looked down. "I wouldn't count on it."

His sister punched him in the arm. "Come on, buck up." She turned to Fanny and her grandmother. "He told me he has his first murder investigation, and I think it's fascinating."

When Peter didn't respond, she punched him again. "I know you'll figure it out, Pete. Be positive, will you?"

He sighed. "My sister is a freshman at Wellesley College," he told Fanny.

"She's a very good student," Cornelia boasted.

"And Gran is the one who put up the money for me to go there, so I'd better be good," Holly said. "My father wouldn't do it."

"I know it's what your mother would have wanted," Cornelia said. It seemed to Fanny that her friend didn't want to encourage criticism of the father.

Fanny decided to change the subject to one she was more interested in. "Peter, how is your investigation going? Did you find the murder weapon?"

"The gun?" Holly asked, bright-eyed and curious.

"Ah, there was a second murder, Hol," Peter told her. "A man found beaten to death. We found an iron pipe and brought it back to Dr. Magrath."

"Two murders. How exciting," Holly smiled. "You'll really make an impression when you solve two murders. Father won't be able to put you down after that."

Peter groaned. "That's assuming we solve them. And that I even stay on the case." He looked at Fanny. "Chief McKenna is going to throw me off the case if I don't arrest someone by Friday. He says he'll make an arrest himself; then he'll probably use my failure to throw me off the detective squad altogether." He frowned and looked around, then spoke softly to Fanny. "He wants me to arrest Bill Callahan."

"Look," Fanny said. "There's Mr. Callahan himself."

Chapter Twenty

Peter turned around to look where Mrs. Lee was staring. Sure enough, there was Mr. Callahan, talking to John F. Fitzgerald, the ex-mayor of Boston who was known as Honey Fitz. They stood in a group of cigar-smoking city men surrounding one of the inductees. Waiters circulated with trays of champagne glasses. Callahan stopped one, and the group all grabbed glasses for a toast.

"Interlopers." Peter's father returned to them, trailed by the man he had been talking to. Peter wanted to roll his eyes but restrained himself. He knew he'd be getting an earful of "I told you so's" from his father soon enough. He recognized the man with his father as a competitor in the sailboat races from the summer.

"Cornelia, Mrs. Lee, I'd like you to meet Augustus Lane Sumner. His father was a classmate of mine at Harvard." Peter thought this was a jab at him for leaving that institution. Most of his father's friends had graduated from Harvard. Sumner must be the owner of the company that Ian Stewart worked for. Meanwhile, Peter's father was disparaging the inductee that Callahan and Honey Fitz were toasting.

"Just another of these rascals," Attwood senior sniffed. "They get into the government offices like mold seeping into plaster. And they spread. I've warned the membership committee, but they insist on a certain number being admitted. The day they induct that crook Curley is the day I resign." He stopped a passing waiter and made sure everyone in the group had champagne. He raised an eyebrow when his daughter lifted a glass, but she turned away strategically while she sipped. His sister always knew how to handle the old man. She knew he'd hate to make a scene in public, even if it meant letting his daughter drink alcohol. Attwood Senior was a "dry." He'd voted for prohibition. But Peter knew he was a hypocrite. He might be "dry" in his politics, but he'd already stocked up his cellar with wines and whiskey so he wouldn't be "dry" at the dinner table when the time came.

Sumner harrumphed. "That's Callahan over there, the son. He'll be the next one getting inducted. He's been trying to get himself nominated for months."

"No!" Peter's father protested. "He's the son of a workman, isn't he?"

"The old man was always a good carpenter," Sumner said, then swallowed the rest of his champagne. "He worked for McKay, you know. He built the company, taking on some jobs I wouldn't want to tackle. But he never tried to weasel his way into society. He was content to do commercial work. Docks and wharves for the big liners. But the son is worming his way into private work. He bid on the docks up at the club, and I think he'll get the contract. It's too small for my company, and he'll sacrifice on price just to get the contact. It's disgusting when you think of it."

"The club?" Attwood cried. Peter could see his father was outraged. The Eastern Yacht Club in Marblehead was sacred to him. He exchanged a look with Holly. His father was so narrow-minded these days.

Sumner shrugged. "Like I said, it's a small job. It doesn't bother me. It's when he goes after the bigger projects, like the proposed tunnel, that I put my foot down. My ancestors were the first ones to develop East Boston. When there's a tunnel being built there, we're the ones who should do it."

Peter wanted to ask Sumner more about the Callahan company and its rivalry with Sumner's company, especially since there had been sabotage at Callahan's. But to do that, he'd have to admit he was a police detective assigned to the murders in the Sumner company's backyard. He knew that would infuriate his father. And his father didn't know he was assigned to investigate those deaths. He would soon enough if Peter got demoted or fired because of them.

Fanny rescued him. "Mr. Sumner, are you aware there have been two murders in East Boston just this week? I believe they happened very close to your company offices."

Attwood senior looked shocked that a lady would mention such topics. Peter saw that his grandmother and Holly were amused by his father's reaction. He knew his grandmother would be totally unfazed by her son-in-law's disapproval. Thank God for Gran. "Well, yes. Of course, my manager has informed me. But it's nothing to do with us," Sumner said. He sniffed.

"I was there with Dr. Magrath, the medical examiner. He's a friend of mine, and I help him sometimes with notes and sketches of crime scenes."

Mrs. Lee continued, unimpressed by the reactions of the men. Peter saw a look of admiration in Holly's eyes. "Mr. Sumner, I heard that the Callahan company has suffered from some accidents that are believed to be sabotage. Have you suffered from that as well?"

Sumner clutched the ornamental sword at his side. "It's not just Callahan's. All the businesses by the wharves have had things stolen, broken, or damaged. You may not be aware, dear lady—Mrs. Lee didn't flinch, but Peter was sure he saw a dangerous glint in her eye at the patronizing tone of the Yankee businessman. "But there are criminals planning to illegally import liquor once prohibition goes into effect, and they want to intimidate any businesses on the waterfront so they can do their dirty work without interference. They're just making everyone aware of what they could do."

Peter looked at him. "You mean they plan to bring in alcohol by boat?"

Peter's father scoffed. "You don't know? There's a man named McCoy who plans to ship wine, beer, and liquor as far as the international line. Then, small boats will go out and get the contraband and sail it to land to sell at a big profit. Are you telling me the police aren't aware of this?" It was the first mention of police Peter had heard from his father that wasn't in a tirade about his son's choices. He obviously didn't think well of them. Peter wondered if his father was aware of the plans to smuggle liquor because he had plans to buy it when it came ashore. He wouldn't be surprised.

Sumner was shaking his head. "As soon as the Volstead Act takes effect, they'll be out there. Anyhow, that's who's terrorizing the waterfront." He nodded toward the group that included Callahan and Fitzgerald. "And if you think that crowd doesn't know about it, you'd be fooling yourself." He glanced across the room. "Come on, Rupert, I see the awards committee from the club having an impromptu meeting over there. I suggest we join them."

Without excusing themselves, the men walked away.

Fanny looked at Peter. "That gives you something to think about, doesn't it?"

It did. But whether that would help him meet his two-day deadline for an arrest was doubtful.

Chapter Twenty-One

Before she and Peter had parted at the end of the Ancients' induction ceremony Fanny had convinced him to meet her at the morgue the next morning so that they could update Jake with their latest findings.

As they waited in the chilly morning breeze, Fanny considered the young man beside her. Tall and gangly with shoulders hunched against the wind, he looked so young. But the young were malleable. She knew that Jake could help him sift through the evidence, and also learn proper methods of investigation. She believed both men needed a prod from her to do what needed to be done. She was aware they would have to fight a stagnant, ingrained system, but it was worth doing. She was already outside that system—a wealthy woman with not enough to do in the view of McKenna and others. But being outside the system gave her the freedom to see that it needed to be torn down and rebuilt. If Peter could solve these cases using Jake's methods, that ought to show McKenna something. Or, more importantly, show McKenna's superiors something.

Edwin admitted them and took them to the big autopsy room. There were no bodies laid out this time. Jake gestured them to stools as he removed his apron. Fanny was glad to see he seemed to expect reports from the young detective.

Peter spilled everything he'd learned, and he described his confrontation with McKenna. Jake rolled his stool to the metal table that was still wet from a washing down. He leaned on his elbows. "So, McKenna wants you to arrest Bill Callahan based on rumors that he had a romantic relationship with the dead woman?"

"Yes, but Mack is adamant that there was nothing going on between them, and he does live there," Peter said.

Fanny thought Peter was afraid of the big Irishman. When Mack was adamant about something, he was also boisterous about it. If Peter actually arrested Callahan, Fanny could imagine Mack getting worked up enough to throw the young detective against a wall. She suspected Peter had the same thought.

Jake looked across to catch Fanny's eye. "There's something you should know about Chief McKenna," he told Peter. "This past winter, his wife was killed. She'd been unfaithful. I'm afraid that personal experience may incline him to believe stories about the dead woman."

"He just wants a quick and easy solution," Fanny scoffed. She thought McKenna was a lazy man.

Jake frowned. "That, too. He'll want to show results to his superiors. Especially since he was so recently promoted."

"I can't believe they promoted him," Fanny said, but Jake waved her comment away. He'd told her before that he didn't approve of denigrating higher authorities in front of the young detective.

"What actual evidence is there that Bill Callahan could have shot Ingrid Ericksson?" Jake asked Peter.

"He was in his office in the building next door, but the door was closed, and his workmen were busy at the docks."

"Does he own a gun?"

"He says not. His father may have an old rifle, but the old man wasn't around when we were there. I haven't spoken to him."

"You should. So, theoretically, Callahan could have shot her. How would that occur? No one saw him, but no one saw anyone else, either," Jake pointed out.

"It's hard to imagine how *anyone* could have shot her," Peter said. "No one was on the porch, because Lars Ericksson was inside and would have seen if someone was there. There's no love lost between the husband and Callahan. Lars accused Callahan but said nothing about him being there. Do you think

Callahan could have come out of the building to shoot her from the ground?"

"Or the roof," Jake suggested. He looked at Fanny. Reluctantly, she drew her sketchpad from her bag and flipped to the page showing the buildings. Peter looked at it carefully.

"So, I should check the roof. Talk with the old man and get the rifle if there is one."

"Where did the bullet go?" Jake asked. "It passed through the body. She was outside, so it could have gone anywhere, but, if you did find it, it could help indicate where the shot came from."

"What about Leary?" Peter asked. "He must have seen something. If he saw Callahan, then the man had to get rid of him, maybe? I talked to his coworkers. They say he was a drunk."

Fanny didn't like how they were concentrating on Bill Callahan. Her dislike of McKenna made her want him to be wrong. "What if Callahan didn't do it?" she asked impatiently. "Last night, we met Augustus Sumner. He said there are gangs planning on bringing in liquor once prohibition goes into effect, and they're behind the accidents and thefts on the wharves. Couldn't they have killed Leary?"

Peter nodded his head. "Yes, I was thinking Leary was around all the time but not doing much, according to the other men. Surely, he could have seen something about the sabotage at Callahan's. Doesn't it seem more likely men like that would beat him to death? Maybe he tried to blackmail someone."

"What about the woman then? Why was Ingrid killed?" Jake asked. He looked satisfied by the way Peter was struggling with the problem.

"I don't know. I suppose she could have seen something, too."

"Or?" Jake prompted.

Peter thought. "Or the two deaths have nothing to do with each other." He hesitated. "Mack thinks the husband killed Ingrid."

"He did have a rifle," Fanny said.

"Even if his wife wasn't involved with Bill Callahan, Lars could have believed she was," Peter said.

"Where's that rifle?" Jake asked.

Hearing movement behind her, Fanny realized Jake's assistant had been standing there. Edwin stepped to a cabinet and brought the rifle out. "It doesn't seem to have been used recently," he said. "It could have been cleaned after the shooting, though." He handed it to Jake.

"Especially since the death was deemed accidental at first," Jake said, examining the gun.

Peter flushed. Fanny kept quiet with an effort. She didn't want Jake to put down the boy when he was already almost in despair.

"Too bad they didn't find the bullet," Edwin said. "I've been reading about some work done to match bullets to specific guns by comparing the marks on the bullets."

"Really?' Peter asked. "You can prove a specific gun was used?"

They all turned their attention to the assistant, who warmed to his topic. Jake had mentioned that in all his studies, Edwin had become obsessed with subjects related to crimes and what was known as legal medicine.

"There was a man condemned to be executed in New York a few years ago," Edwin told them. "The governor stayed the execution while scientists investigated. They were able to prove the man's gun couldn't have fired the bullets that killed his neighbors. A New York lab worked on that comparison."

"Now, that's very interesting," Jake said, proud of his protégé.

Fanny detected a kindred spirit in Edwin. Like her, he wanted to complete the stories of the lives that had animated the bodies he saw on the morgue tables. Fanny shared the young assistant's urge to explain those deaths. They had both gotten the urge by watching Jake, who was meticulous about such explanations.

Peter was excited. "That's fantastic."

"Except we don't have the bullet," Jake pointed out drily.

"We should have looked for that from the beginning," Peter almost wailed. He knew he had flubbed up yet again.

"Um-hmm," Jake muttered. Fanny knew that Jake despaired of getting police investigators to spend the time and effort needed at a crime scene, but she thought he was too pessimistic. Here was a young detective ready to listen and learn. Of course, if he didn't solve the crime, he might lose his gold badge. That was an issue they needed to address. Peter had to succeed.

"Let's go back to East Boston," Fanny said.

Chapter Twenty-Two

Peter wasn't at all sure it was a good idea to take Mrs. Lee along when he returned to East Boston. But she was a strong-willed woman and experience with his grandmother and sister had taught him it was useless to fight female stubbornness. She gamely took the subway with him. Built in 1904, the streetcars traversed the first-ever tunnel under the harbor to get to East Boston. It was still a marvel to someone like Mrs. Lee, who rode the cars for the first time.

At Maverick Square, she immediately entered a taxi, beckoning Peter to follow. "Don't worry, I'll pay," she reassured him.

The taxi dropped them on Border Street in the alley between the Callahan and Sumner companies.

"We'll look for the bullet first," Peter said. He needed to take the reins now that they were at the crime scene. He didn't want to be led around like a child. Mrs. Lee pursed her lips and nodded, letting him take the lead.

There was no sign of Mack when they entered the three-decker. They could hear Kate and her children on the second floor. Peter stopped at the third floor to knock.

The door was opened by a red-eyed Lars Ericksson. A child of about two years clutched his leg. This must be Lilly, the daughter.

"Excuse me, Mr. Ericksson, but I need to search your porch once more," Peter felt his face redden. Ericksson might not know how incompetent he was in having failed to search for the bullet earlier, but Peter was painfully aware of it.

The big Swede let him brush past, and Peter heard Mrs. Lee greet him and ask about the little girl. Perhaps it was good she had come. She could distract him.

On the porch, Peter looked for any sign of the bullet that had passed through Ingrid Ericksson. Where could it have gone? He peered out at the steep hill to the left where the Callahan house and others backed onto the front yard of the three-decker. The warehouses of Callahan and Sumner stood to his right. It was a huge area. Peter despaired of finding the bullet. It could have gone anywhere. Would he have to tramp all over the yard and buildings looking for it?

Mack thought Ericksson had killed his wife. Since they'd already taken the rifle from the husband, it would be a neat solution to find the bullet and have Edwin match it to Ericksson's rifle. If Ingrid had stood looking out as Peter did now, facing the railing, the bullet from the gun would have gone out into the wild of the yard. But what if she'd stood on one of the chairs, hanging laundry? Where would the bullet go? Could it have gone into the walls of the porch?

Reluctantly, Peter began to search the floor of the porch inch by inch. Nothing. He moved rickety chairs and scrutinized the wooden siding. The paint flaked, but he found no bullet. He diligently traced the walls up and down until he saw something in the ceiling. Surely that couldn't be...

The bottom of the roof that extended over the porch formed the ceiling. Made of old wooden planks in fairly good condition, he could see they were protected from the weather. Peter glimpsed a mark in the wood. He pulled one of the chairs over and climbed up. It shook with his weight, and he grabbed at the wall to steady himself, giving a yelp in the process.

Ericksson and Mrs. Lee rushed out. "What's going on? Are you all right?" Mrs. Lee asked.

Ericksson frowned at him. "Get down from there."

Peter balanced precariously, pointing up. "I think I found it, but I can't reach."

Ericksson took a step forward. Peter could see the big man was angry, but Mrs. Lee put a hand on his arm. "Mr. Ericksson, I believe the detective may have found the bullet that killed your wife. Do you think you could help us dig it out to take back to Dr. Magrath? As I told you, he's my friend, and he's trying to find the truth of what happened to your wife."

Peter was concerned that Mrs. Lee stood so close to the very angry man. After all, Mack believed the Swede had killed his wife. Peter knew Dr. Magrath would never forgive him if Mrs. Lee were harmed. He jumped down, keenly aware that he was no match for the huge man. Mrs. Lee had made a mistake in telling Ericksson they were looking for evidence. Peter trusted Mack's instincts and had little confidence in his own since he knew he lacked the ex-detective's experience. He never should have let Mrs. Lee accompany him.

But Mrs. Lee tamed the angry Swede. He abruptly turned back into the house and came back out with a step ladder and a hunting knife. Peter stepped in front of Mrs. Lee at the sight of the knife, but Ericksson just brushed past, shoving the rickety chair away as he placed the ladder and climbed up. He used the knife to dig something out, then jumped down and held out his big hand. It was the bullet.

Chapter Twenty-Three

Fanny carefully wrapped the evidence in the brown paper she got from Ericksson. She could sense that Peter was wary of the big Swede, but she had talked to the sorrowful widower while Peter searched, and she had her own doubts about his guilt. She thought that Peter agreed with Mack that Callahan had nothing to do with Ingrid Ericksson's death. She knew the young detective was being pressured to arrest Callahan, but she suspected he was a little too eager to prove his superior, Captain McKenna, wrong. Caught between the beliefs of the older men, Peter was too hesitant to trust his own unproven instincts. She would also like to see McKenna proved wrong, but she kept an open mind on the idea that the dead woman could have been killed by a lover. And that lover could have been the wealthy businessman from next door.

In any case, she needed a carpenter, and Lars was a good one. She didn't need to share her plans with Peter. He was already anxious about her presence and felt obliged to protect her. He wouldn't approve of the agreement she'd made with Ericksson while Peter was on the porch.

"I need to talk to the elder Mr. Callahan," Peter said. She knew he'd like to send her back to Beacon Hill, but she had no intention of returning without him. "To ask about a rifle," he reminded her.

"Yes, let's go. Thank you for your help, Mr. Ericksson, and goodbye, Lilly. I hope I'll see you again." She had made friends with the motherless two-year-old who clung to her father's leg again. "You be a good girl for your father now."

She followed Peter down to the yard, where they found a set of stairs that took them up the steep hillside to Meridian Street above. They turned left up the sidewalk to reach the double doors of the Callahan row house, but this time, they rang the bell on the right. The building was split down the middle for the Callahan father and son.

A young maid answered and ushered them into a large study at the back of the house. William Callahan senior had a view of the docks out his back window just as his son had in the office next door. His desk faced the windows and had far fewer papers than his son's. Instead, woodworking tools and curls of wood shavings littered the desktop. He'd been whittling a child's toy, a horse.

Old Will Callahan stood over six feet, with broad shoulders and defined muscles in his arms. He turned toward them as they entered. Fanny saw he was less formal in his dress than his son. He wore suspenders over a linen shirt with the sleeves rolled up. He had a head of straight white hair. He wore it slightly longer than was usual, with a side part and he had a flourishing full beard. Brown eyes gleamed deep in a wrinkled face. Fanny thought he looked rather stony, like the granite rocks on her New Hampshire estate.

Peter introduced himself and explained that he was investigating the deaths of Mrs. Ericksson and Conor Leary. He stumbled as he introduced Fanny as a friend of Dr. Magrath, and she gritted her teeth. She'd have to speak to him about how to introduce her. She was an associate, after all, not just a friend.

Old Will turned out to be a man of few words. Fanny looked around as Peter tried to pry information from the elder Callahan. Handsome mahogany bookcases lined one wall but held few books. On a side table, a beautifully carved chess set was laid out with a game in progress. A bowl of chrysanthemums sat on a varnished buffet while a few metal tools lay on a wide table in the corner. Will motioned them to sit on leather chairs with bronze studs, which Fanny found quite comfortable.

Will himself roamed restlessly between the desk and the visitor chairs, staring out the windows most of the time. Peter had elicited a few yays and nays from the man, but he was getting to the meat of the matter now.

"Mr. Callahan, you knew Ingrid Ericksson, the dead woman. Were you aware of a connection between her and your son Bill?"

"No."

Peter waited for more, but nothing came. Finally, he asked. "Is it true that you are friendly with Mr. Lars Ericksson and that you frequently visit his home?"

"Aye."

"How is it you're so friendly with your employee?"

"Good carpenter. Plays chess."

Peter paused, obviously hoping for more but silence reigned. Fanny hoped the young man wouldn't lose his temper. "Is it true that your son, Bill, also frequently visited the Ericksson home?"

"To call me to dinner."

"And was he particularly friendly with Mrs. Ericksson when he went there?"

Old Will gave Peter a glassy stare, finally replying, "He's a deal friendly with everybody. It's his way."

"I understand. But, you see, Mr. Ericksson has accused your son of having a relationship with his wife." Fanny could see that Peter was trying to provoke the old man. She didn't think he'd have any luck with that. Exasperated, Peter pushed on. "Was there a romantic attachment between them, as Mr. Ericksson believes?"

"No. Naught of that."

It was a final pronouncement. Peter seemed a bit stumped. He cleared his throat. "Do you or your son own a rifle?"

Silence.

"Sir? Did you hear me?"

"Aye. I'm not deaf yet. There's a rifle."

"Could I see it?" Silence. "Sir?"

Without a word, Old Will trudged out of the room. Peter looked at Fanny and threw up his hands.

"Just wait," she told him.

Sure enough, the old man trudged back into the room with a rifle in his hands. "Don't worry, I checked. It's not loaded," he said as he handed it to

Peter.

"A twenty-two," Peter looked over at Fanny with triumph. Fanny was glad they had the bullet that she had carefully placed in her bag. Now, they had two guns and a bullet to match them to. Edwin would be able to do his scientific comparison, and the truth would out no matter which man was responsible. She thought it was progress.

Peter turned the rifle over in his hands. She thought it was dawning on him that he might have to arrest the younger Callahan after all.

"Is your son home or in his warehouse today?" Peter asked.

Another glassy stare from the old man. "Marblehead. Dock there. Reception tonight."

The remark seemed cryptic to Fanny, but Peter was able to interpret it.

"Ah, yes, there's the awards dinner up there tonight," Peter said. He glanced across at Fanny. "My father sails out of Eastern Yacht Club in Marblehead," he explained. He turned back to Old Will. "We heard that your company might get the contract for a new dock up there. Is that why your son is there?"

"Aye." The old man blinked. "Mighty small deal, but Bill's keen."

"Yes, I see. We'll have to borrow this rifle for now. And there's one more thing. You must have heard that Conor Leary was found beaten to death in a bin beside your warehouse. Do you have any idea who could have done that? Did he have enemies?"

Old Will stopped pacing and folded his arms on his chest, staring down at the floor. "Sad man," he said finally. "Poor Conor. Gone to drink. No one to stop him. Wife threw him out. Can't blame her. Jealous old soul. Sad soul." He sighed.

Peter jumped on the man's comment. "He was jealous? Who was he jealous of?"

Will looked at him through bleary eyes. Fanny thought the old stone face was near tears.

"Everyone," he answered. "Thought everyone had done better than him. Especially Bill. So much younger. So much better off."

Peter perked up. "Do you think he could have been responsible for the sabotage your firm has been experiencing?" Fanny thought it was a good question.

"He were too dumb for that." Will shook his head. "That's them, rumrunners, I bet. I told Bill, you just got to let them go their way, and we go ours. It's none of our business now."

"You mean the sabotage was a warning not to interfere with them? Do you think they could have beaten Leary?" Peter was excited by the prospect of new suspects.

The old man dropped his arms to his sides. "I've no knowledge of that. Now, if that's all, I have work to be doing."

"What's all this?" A woman in her thirties wearing a fur-trimmed coat and a tall hat walked into the room. "Pa, who are you talking to?"

Before Fanny could guess who she was, Peter spoke. "Mrs. Callahan. I'm Detective Attwood, if you recall. This is Mrs. Lee. We were asking your father-in-law a few questions about the deaths we're investigating."

Chapter Twenty-Four

So, this was Eileen Callahan. Fanny had heard Peter describe the scene between Bill Callahan's wife and Lars Ericksson. Eileen narrowed her eyes in suspicion as she held out a gloved hand to Fanny and Peter. She was a large-framed woman who softened her look with a delicate fluff of lace that fell down the front of her blouse. She didn't need the extra height of the tall hat, but Fanny recognized it as the newest style this year. Eileen wasn't pretty; her mouth was too wide and her nose too big, but she compensated for that by wearing elegant clothes and projecting a vital energy.

After a doubtful glance at her father-in-law, Eileen stared at the rifle in Peter's hands.

He looked uncomfortable. "We need to examine it," he said, attempting to hide the gun by lowering it to his side. He blushed. "I know you believe there was nothing between Mrs. Ericksson and your husband, but we have to consider every possibility."

"Well, you're barking up the wrong tree," she told him. She turned a shoulder to him, to face Fanny. "Mrs. Lee, Kate Gallagher mentioned you to me. She said you're working with the police. How did you come to do such work?"

"Actually, I'm working with the medical examiner, Dr. Magrath. He investigates the circumstances of a death and shares the evidence and his conclusions with the police. I take notes and do drawings for him as necessary." Eileen's eyes raked over her, looking for a way to place her. It must be obvious to her that Fanny wasn't a working woman. "Dr. Magrath is an old friend of my family," Fanny admitted.

"I see." Eileen stared at the rifle Peter held at his side. "We're all deeply sorry for Ingrid's passing. She has a young daughter, and her husband is out of his mind with grief. But there's no reason any of us would have wanted to harm the poor woman. Lars is a fine worker and a friend to my father-in-law. They play chess all the time." She pulled off her coat and gloves to sling them onto the sofa. "If you're looking for Bill, Detective Attwood, he's not here. He's gone up to Marblehead to talk about a contract. I came to invite Pa to dinner with us." She sat down on the sofa, carefully removing her hat and patting it fondly as she set it on the side table.

Old Will smiled at his daughter-in-law. The hard lines of his face softened, looking at her. Fanny guessed the young woman could twist the older man around her finger.

Eileen smiled back. "Billy and Sister will be home. Agnes is cooking mutton." She shoved a barrette in her hair as she turned toward Fanny. "My children. Billy's eight, and Sister is six. She's named after me, but Billy always calls her 'Sister,' so it stuck." She grinned.

"Where were you?" Will asked. He probably missed her sunny presence when she was out. Fanny suspected the old man was no longer involved in the day-to-day work of the company and might have been lonely in his big house.

"Meetings. Covering meetings. The St. Vincent Society, the Cunard Club." She looked at Fanny. "I'm a sort of reporter." She ignored Peter. "Our paper, *East Boston Free Press,* covers local news and events the big Boston papers don't report. I write up the social events."

Fanny understood. The big papers had similar columns covering events sponsored by the Brahmin ladies. Fundraisers, social clubs, amateur theatrics were all acceptable ways for the ladies to get their names in the papers. The Boston papers didn't report on activities of Roman Catholic societies, at least not those that the ladies participated in. Fanny thought it was spunky of Eileen to create her own social column unfettered by strictures of the old guard. She knew her Brahmin friend, Cornelia, would be amused and would cheer Eileen's efforts. Cornelia also admired spunk, especially in a woman faced with a dominant male society.

Apparently, Eileen was as vehement in her pursuit of social position and connections as her husband was of political institutions like the Ancient and Honorables. Were those ambitions strong enough for a young wife to ignore illicit affairs of her husband? Perhaps. Fanny knew such infidelity would be unacceptable to the ladies' groups where Eileen preened herself. Fanny had struggled in her own marriage, finally ending it with the divorce. But there had been no hint of infidelity. Still, she knew the inner workings of a marriage were not visible to outsiders. Eileen might protect her husband's reputation with others, but Fanny knew that didn't mean she didn't blame him privately. Even if he was innocent, the whiff of scandal was unpleasant.

How dangerous was the threat of scandal to her husband and herself? Boston could be a treacherous place for a young couple like the Callahans who wanted to climb out of the obscurity of an immigrant past into the public life of the city. It wasn't an easy thing to do.

Fanny decided on a direct approach. "Do you have any idea who might have shot Ingrid Ericksson?"

Peter looked embarrassed. Eileen sat up straight. Fanny could imagine the young woman being called to task by a stern nun. She was sure Eileen must have attended one of the local academies for Catholic girls, all run by convents.

"No, of course I don't," Eileen said. Her eyes looked straight ahead, and Fanny saw Old Will's brow wrinkle in a frown. Did he believe her? He pursed his lips and said nothing. "I must be getting home for our meal," she said, standing to gather her coat and hat. "You'll be coming, Pa, won't you?"

Will's face froze. "No. Not tonight. Tonight, South Boston."

Fanny saw Eileen's face redden. "Oh, Pa, the kids will miss you." She grimaced.

Will was immovable. "Tomorrow, maybe."

Eileen sighed. Fanny felt sorry for her and was surprised that Old Will wouldn't dine with his family. She could see he was fond of his daughter-in-law. Eileen's husband was out politicking, and her father-in-law had his own affairs. She was left with her children. What was so important to the old man that he denied her his company? This family, like all families, had secrets. But Fanny couldn't know if those secrets had any bearing on the murders.

"I'll call Maizie to come over," Eileen said. Maizie must be a friend. Fanny could tell it wasn't the first time Eileen had called on a friend to fill in for a missing husband and father-in-law. "I'm sorry we can't help you, Mrs. Lee, Detective Attwood, but our family has nothing to do with poor Ingrid's death." Eileen's eyes lit on the rifle Peter was still trying to conceal at his side. "That's Pa's gun, by the way. Bill never used it. Well, goodbye."

After she rushed away, Fanny could see their welcome was wearing thin with the stolidly silent Old Will. Finally, Peter got the message, and he ushered her out of the house. On the street, he hailed a taxi for Fanny. Helping her in, he handed her the rifle, which she took awkwardly. "Aren't you coming back?"

"No. You have the bullet and the rifle. Can you make sure they get to Dr. Magrath tonight?"

"Yes, of course, but where are you going?" She would have expected him to rush Edwin into a comparison to find out which gun matched the bullet from the porch. It was Friday, Chief McKenna's deadline for Peter to make an arrest. Was he giving up?

"I'm going to Marblehead. It's all right. My father and brother will be there. I was supposed to attend." He made a face. "I need to talk to Bill Callahan. I need to understand why Mack insists Callahan didn't have a relationship with Ingrid Ericksson. I don't know where Mack is, but I need to talk to Callahan alone, anyhow."

Fanny could see he was torn between two theories of the crime. Mack insisted Lars was guilty. But Chief McKenna wanted Peter to arrest young Callahan. She thought the young detective might be too inexperienced. He didn't know what to do. She sighed as he shut the door and rushed away.

Fanny wanted to find out which gun had fired the shot that killed Ingrid Ericksson. The truth might disappoint Peter if it proved Mack wrong, but she was experienced enough to know the world would go on whichever gun was the murder weapon. She sighed to think of Peter's youth. Disillusionment was part of any young person's education.

Chapter Twenty-Five

Mack pounded on the door of the morgue until Edwin let him in. The ex-detective rushed into Jake's office and planted himself in a hard chair in front of the desk, demanding to know the state of the investigation. Jake told him that Chief Detective McKenna planned to arrest Bill Callahan unless Peter found another suspect by the end of the day. This day. Friday.

"No, no, no! It's all wrong!" Mack yelled, raising his arms in protest.

"Detective Attwood and Mrs. Lee went to interview the elder Mr. Callahan, but they haven't returned. I told them to try to find out if Bill Callahan had access to a rifle," Jake said. It was curious how vehemently Mack defended the younger Callahan. Jake hadn't thought they were especially friendly.

Mack squeezed his eyes closed as he shook his head back and forth. His big hands clutched his knees. "It's not Bill. I keep trying to tell you. And even if the old man has a rifle, there's no reason Bill'd shoot poor Ingrid."

Jake wondered if Mack already knew of a rifle in the Callahan household. He could see the man was bubbling up to a full head of steam. Before Mack could go off on a rant about how Bill Callahan was innocent, Jake decided to distract the stubborn ex-detective.

"Edwin is working on a way to identify exactly which rifle shot a specific bullet. He'll compare the markings on two fired bullets to see if they match. He's setting up a test out in the garage. Of course, it's of no use unless they find the bullet that killed Ingrid Ericksson."

Mack had sizzled down a bit as he tried to puzzle through what Jake said.

"Come on out and take a look." Jake got up and led the way to the drafty garage, where a truck was parked in one bay, and another was empty. It wasn't a bad idea to have the experienced detective take a look at Edwin's procedures.

Overhead lights cast a stark light on the cement box. Edwin, who usually retreated into shadowy corners, was illuminated. The burn scars on his face were impossible to ignore, and Mack was never subtle.

"God Almighty, you're a sight, aren't you then?"

Edwin froze, and Jake's heart went out to him. The damaged veteran hated to be reminded of the ruin of his face. Mack was such a blunderer.

"You'll be scaring the girls away with a puss like that, won't you?"

Jake was so horrified he was stunned to silence. Edwin had crept out of his shell in recent months since he began his medical studies. Jake wanted to slap Mack for blithely destroying the confidence that Jake had tried so hard to build in his young assistant.

To Jake's surprise, Edwin unfroze and turned to face Mack head-on, giving him a good look at the scars. Jake couldn't stand it. "Edwin was burned by a bomb in the trenches of France," he said, hoping to embarrass Mack.

The big man didn't flinch at the sight of Edwin's face. "That must've hurt. You're a brave man to take it. Now that's a quality that will attract the lasses. And it's great for getting their sympathy, too. You ex-soldiers have got a jump on those of us who didn't fight, that's for sure, you lucky dumb muck."

Edwin took a big breath and rolled his eyes. He turned back to a tall bench where he'd set up two microscopes. Jake knew Edwin was "walking out" with a young widow who had worked for Fanny. He thought of mentioning that to Mack, who seemed to be ruefully unattached himself, but that was Edwin's business, so Jake kept his peace. "Edwin, show us what you're working on."

Edwin explained that he planned to compare markings on bullets shot from different guns. He pulled a small rifle from a shelf. "This is the gun you took from Lars Ericksson. We need to shoot and retrieve a bullet. Then, if Detective Attwood finds the bullet that killed Ingrid Ericksson, we can compare them." He walked to the other side of the empty bay. A box was set on edge on top of a tall stool. "I've packed this with mud, and I'll discharge into it." He aimed at the box.

"No!" Mack yelled, but it was too late. The ear-shattering bang of a gunshot echoed in the cement garage, and ricochets dinged twice before the noise stopped.

Mack had dived to the ground, Jake threw his hands up, and Edwin stood with his mouth open.

"Jesus, Mary, and Joseph!" Mack jumped to his feet and grabbed the gun from Edwin. Jake's ears still rang with the shot. Mack shouted, all of them temporarily deafened from the noise, "You're too close, man. Much too close."

Edwin was crestfallen as Mack examined the box. The bullet had passed through the mud and out the back. It left a hole in the wood of the packing box, then slammed the cement walls before dropping.

Edwin searched the floor and found a smashed bullet near Jake. He held it up in dismay. It was too misshapen to show any markings. Mack watched him.

"Christ, man, what were you thinking? You were a soldier. Don't you know better?" Mack yelled.

Edwin looked abashed. "I guess we were always outside when we shot. I didn't think." His face turned a deep red. Jake supposed it was true. As a soldier, Edwin would have been trained and fought in open spaces. Mack, on the other hand, as a city cop, would have more experience with close quarters. Jake had only ever shot off a gun on hunting trips. Although he'd seen the result of indoor gunshots on dead bodies, he hadn't been present when the gun went off.

"Lucky you missed the doctor. You'd be out of a job. Got to be careful in a cement box like this." Mack waved a big hand around. He noticed how downcast Edwin was. "You can still do it, you know." He held up the gun. "All you need is some distance, see." Stepping to the table, he pulled back the bolt and reloaded the gun. "And more to stop the bullet." Jake watched with apprehension as Mack set the mud-filled packing box back on the stool. Then he pulled over another stool and set it up in front. Grabbing another box made of two by fours, he put that on the second stool. After eyeing his work, Mack paced out seven or eight steps back from it. Jake put up a hand to stop him.

"You might want to wait inside the door," Mack waved the muzzle in that direction. "This should work, but if you get a ricochet again, it might not miss you this time. No sense pressing your luck." He grinned.

Jake and Edwin took his advice. Jake wasn't sure it was safe for the shooter either, but he could tell from the gleam in Mack's eye that any objection would be futile. They shut the door, which muffled the shot. Then they stepped back in.

Mack was at the box with the mud, fiddling with a knife. "Here you go!" He handed a muddied ball to Edwin, who grabbed it, excited to rub off the mud. Taking it to one of the microscopes, he centered it and looked. "You can see it." He moved away and offered the eyepiece to Jake. The microscope enlarged the small bullet, and Jake could see markings on the sides.

Mack was less than impressed. "So? Scratches?"

Edwin elbowed him aside and began drawing the bullet in a notepad. "The point is that any bullet from this gun will have the same marks, while a bullet from a different gun will have different markings. You see?"

Mack's brow furrowed. "You can say which gun shot Ingrid?"

Jake sighed. "Only if you have the bullet that shot her. It went through her and out her front, so we don't have it to compare."

Mack frowned with impatience. "That gun was from Lars, right? He's sure to be the one who shot her. He's a hard man, that Lars."

They heard a knock on the street door. Since Edwin was busy sketching the bullet, Jake marched over to open it. Fanny hurried in. "Where's Detective Attwood?" Jake asked.

"He went to a yacht club dinner," she said as she trooped in carrying a gun and a carpet bag. "But we found it. Not the gun." She thrust the rifle at Jake. "This gun is from Bill Callahan's father." Digging into the bag, she pulled out a brown paper-wrapped package. "We think this is the bullet that killed Ingrid Ericsson."

Chapter Twenty-Six

Peter hugged himself as he walked up the gravel drive to the Eastern Yacht Club in Marblehead. He liked the sharp smell of seaweed, but the air had a bite to it. At least there was no wind. The sky was clear with a multitude of stars flung across a velvet backdrop. He'd spent many busy days on the grounds of Eastern Yacht Club growing up, but he'd seldom walked there when the trees had dropped all their leaves, and the docks to his left were mostly empty. Windows of the big gray shingled clubhouse up the hill were lit up, and he could hear piano music spilling out.

He sniffed. A tangy smell tickled his nose. Not a wood fire, something more aromatic. He stopped. A large sloop was knocking gently against the dock to his left, and he could hear the tinkle of halyards on the mast. Only two or three small boats were moored in the harbor. Most had been sailed to boatyards for the winter. Peter turned down the hill and stepped onto the floating dock. He felt it shift with his weight. "Hello," he called.

The dock rocked as a figure trundled down toward him. He recognized Ian Stewart, the manager of the Sumner company. The pipe Peter had smelled was locked in his teeth, and he carried a large bag over his shoulder. "Hallo to you," he greeted Peter.

"Have you been sailing?" Peter asked. His eyes swept up the tall mast of the big boat, empty now, the sail packed away somewhere. The sloop reminded him of the denuded trees along the path. It was too late in the season to be sailing.

Ian swung the bag down and took the pipe out of his mouth. "Aye, just bringing her up for Mr. Sumner. I take it he's selling her."

"Selling? I'm surprised." Peter recognized the yacht as the *Eagle*, a boat that had beaten his father's in many races. "It's a winner, that boat. Why would he sell it?"

Ian shrugged. "Ours is not to reason why. I'd say he must be buying a better boat."

Peter thought his own father would be jealous and the sale of the *Eagle* would force him to buy a new boat. Peter promised himself he wouldn't crew for his father next summer. That was over for him. His thoughts turned back to Ian. "How was the sail? Cold?"

"Aye, and a bit wet, although we waited for the wind to die down before coming. Got use from the oilskins." He patted the big bag.

"Are you coming up to the clubhouse?" Peter asked.

Ian folded his arms and spoke around the pipe. "No, no, we've just brought the boat. We'll be catching the train back to the city." Peter could see a twinkle in the man's eye in the moonlight. "We're not to be mixing with the high and mighty. You'll be, though, will ye?"

Peter felt embarrassed. He'd like to invite the manager to the warmth of the party, but he knew his father wouldn't approve. A good thing he didn't have Mack in tow. That big Irishman would really be impossible to explain. He wouldn't fit in with the yacht club men. "I've got to meet my father and brother up there," he said, nodding at the clubhouse.

At that moment, a shiny Ford rushed by. Ian squinted. "I know that motorcar. He's got a raccoon tail flying from the back. It's young Callahan."

"I think he's bidding on some dock work for the club," Peter said. It seemed rude that Callahan was joining the party, while Ian, who'd had a wet ride up from the city, was excluded. The Sumner manager chuckled.

"Aye, a small job, too small for us, I heard. Sumner's after a much bigger one. A tunnel they're planning now. He's been getting us to prepare for that one. There's a big vote on it next week." He hoisted the bag on his shoulder again. "Well, I'll be off to catch my train with my men. You'd best go up and see your father then." Chewing on his pipe, he walked away toward town.

Peter reluctantly slogged up the road to the clubhouse, arriving just as Bill Callahan was greeted by the club's commodore. Peter recognized Augustus

Lane Sumner, Ian's employer, in the group of men who led Bill away for discussion. They were on the board of the club. He vaguely recalled that Sumner was due to become commodore the next spring. Peter's father would be livid when that happened. Outwardly friendly, the men were bitter rivals who dueled it out on the water. The title of commodore was mostly honorary at the club, but grown men like Sumner and Peter's father vied for bragging rights. 'Commodore!' It wasn't like they led a fighting navy, for heaven's sake. Peter saw his father frowning at him from across the room and dutifully joined him and his brother.

Drinks in hand, his father's group was discussing the English boat *Shamrock IV* that had been shipped to New York in preparation for the America's Cup trials in the spring. The controversy was whether or not the American sloop *Resolute* would change to a Marconi rig. The new invention was a strictly triangular sail that got rid of the boom-like gaff of wood along the top of the mainsail. The English boat came with two full rigs, gaff, and the new Marconi. Spring on the water tests would decide which would be used in the big race. Peter left them to the technical discussion and headed to the bar for a drink. Notes from a popular song about blowing bubbles played on the club piano tinkled in the background.

He noticed the board members who surrounded Bill Callahan looked satisfied with their discussion. Peter knew his father would object to the newcomer being chosen for the project, but Peter's father was no longer on the board.

Ignoring a brief glare from his father, Peter wandered over to the group around Callahan. Augustus Lane Sumner, known as "Gus" around the club, raised his glass when he recognized Peter. "How are you, young man?"

He was a tall, gangly man with bulging eyes and a foolish expression on his face. Peter was sure that while Sumner recognized him, he didn't remember his name. No one could imagine how Sumner managed to win so many races. Peter's father had scoffed, pointing out that Sumner hired a champion sailing coach to manage the boat for him. Sumner was always on the boat but not always at the helm. He was more comfortable in the Adirondack chairs on the club porch, reviewing the strategies over a gin and tonic. His highest ambition was to be Commodore.

"I understand you're looking to sell the *Eagle*. Do you mind if I ask why?" Peter asked him.

"Yes, well, that's a new development," Sumner said, sidling up to Peter to keep the conversation between them. He put an arm around Peter's shoulder and steered him away from the small crowd around Callahan. Peter couldn't resist without making a scene. "Have you heard about Herreshoff's newest sloop? It's called S-class. One-design. Twenty-seven feet, huge main, small jib. All the rage."

Peter thought his own father would have to buy an S-boat when he heard Sumner's plan. Another reason not to crew the next season. At least he would have news for his father when he rejoined him. He got the impression that Sumner didn't want to advertise the fact that he was selling the *Eagle*. Peter's father would want to chew on that move.

Escaping Sumner, Peter managed to work his way over to Bill Callahan. A carnation in his buttonhole, Bill was happily accepting congratulations for the contract to rebuild one of the biggest docks of the club. He promised to have it ready in the spring. When he recognized Peter, he stuttered for a moment, but regained his balance before greeting the detective. Peter explained he sailed at the club with his father. Bill relaxed after that.

"I met your wife today," Peter told him when they were away from the larger group. "At your father's."

Bill's face lit up. "Eileen. She'll have been after Pa to come for dinner since I was out. She doesn't like it when he goes off to South Boston." Looking self-conscious, as if he'd spoken out of line, he hurried on. "I was sorry to have to leave her, but she knows it's just business. Anyway," he added in a low voice, "if you've seen her, you'd know there's no reason I'd be seeing another woman. Certainly not Ingrid Ericksson. Eileen and I are partners. Perfect partners."

Peter thought the man was telling the truth. While Eileen Callahan was no beauty, he obviously adored her. No wonder Mack disdained the idea that Bill was romantically involved with the dead woman. But maybe there was another reason. "I've been working with Mack, ex-detective McNally.

He's a friend of yours, isn't he?"

Bill looked confused. "I know him and his brothers, of course. They rent the bottom floor of a three-decker from us, along with his sister. I wouldn't say I'm especially friendly, though. Why do you ask?"

Now Peter was confused. Because Mack had defended Bill, Peter assumed they were friends. But Bill didn't seem to realize it was Mack's insistence that had kept him from being arrested for Ingrid's murder so far. He didn't know that he was in danger of arrest by McKenna. Peter was surprised Mack hadn't warned Bill. "Your father had a rifle, a twenty-two, like the one used to shoot Mrs. Ericksson. We took it away for examination." Perhaps because of Mack's vehement defense of Bill, Peter felt he should warn him how close to the edge he was.

"What?" His head shot up. "What do you mean? That old gun he uses to shoot rabbits? For heaven's sake, I've never even fired it." Suddenly, he seemed to understand the implication. "You can't believe I'd hurt Ingrid. It's absurd."

"Do you know of anyone else who had a reason to hurt her? Her husband?"

"I can't believe Lars would hurt her. He's very quiet, not emotional, and Ingrid was more…excitable, I'd say. But Lars was devoted to her and their little girl. We all thought it was an accident."

"If she'd died from the fall, it could have been. But she was shot." Peter was frustrated. He'd hoped Bill could give him some clue as to who could have killed Ingrid, but he wouldn't even consider the husband.

"What about Conor Leary?" Peter asked.

"Well, that's different. Conor was an old pal of my father's, but he drank too much to be useful. My father insisted on keeping him on the payroll. They knew each other from way back." Bill shook his head. "He was a troublemaker. The truth is he was jealous of my father's success. He was jealous of anyone's success. And he got friendly with some questionable young guys over in South Boston. Drinking as much as he did, I think he'd be hard-pressed to survive once the Volstead Act goes into effect. I expect those guys will find a way around it."

"Who were the men in South Boston?" Peter asked.

CHAPTER TWENTY-SIX

Bill looked uneasy. "The Gustin Gang."

"The Gustin Gang? They're a nasty bunch," Peter said. When he'd worked for Chief Sullivan, Peter had heard of the notorious group, also known as the "Tailboard Thieves," for hijacking delivery trucks stopped at intersections. So far, they had avoided jail time because they hired well-connected lawyers. They seemed far more likely to beat a man to death than Bill. Peter thought he would take this information to McKenna. Surely, he'd be interested in connecting the known criminals to the deaths. He'd tell his superintendent on Monday, and perhaps that would be enough to keep him from arresting Bill Callahan. Peter saw his father frowning at him. "Excuse me, I've got to get back to my family."

Of course, his father already knew all about S-boats and had already ordered one.

Chapter Twenty-Seven

"Whats the verdict? Do they match?" Jake asked.

Fanny shivered. It was cold in the cement garage, but she wanted to see the results of the test. Edwin had cleaned up the bullet that killed Ingrid Ericksson. He'd told them that it was somewhat squashed, whether from entering the wood or some other reason. He'd spent some time carefully cleaning and lining that bullet up under the lens of a microscope until he was satisfied. He peered at it now through one of the microscopes on the tall table against the wall. At the second microscope, he alternated looking at the bullets from the gun they took from Lars Ericksson and the gun she'd brought from the Callahan home.

Mack paced back and forth, a rifle swinging from his hand, making everyone uncomfortable with his sizzling energy, while Edwin compared the markings on the three bullets.

Jake was keeping the peace by force of character. He'd made it clear to the big ex-detective that this was his morgue, and they would proceed in a scientific manner to compare the bullets. He explained to the more attentive Fanny that this kind of comparison had not been used much in court trials, so they wanted to be very careful to do it in a way that could be repeated as necessary.

"There." Edwin lifted his head. "Look."

They gathered around him to look at the two notebook pages where he had drawn what he saw in each microscope. He had three different drawings for each bullet. To Fanny, it appeared they were very different.

"Excuse me, madam." Mack gently pushed her aside. "What does it mean?"

he demanded.

Jake spoke up. "They don't match. We don't have the rifle that fired the shot."

"The rifle we got from Lars Ericksson didn't kill his wife," Edwin said.

Mack groaned and stamped across the room.

"You should be glad the poor woman wasn't killed by her own husband," Jake pointed out.

Mack resumed pacing. "I was sure that cold bastard must have done it. Who else could it be?" He paced faster.

"The Callahan gun didn't kill her either," Edwin said.

Fanny braced for an outbreak from Mack. But when she glanced at the big Irishman, he had sunk down on a stool, the rifle pointed at the ground between his legs. He looked defeated. Heaving himself up, he ran a large hand over his face and sighed. "I'll be off then. I need something after all that."

She assumed he meant a strong drink. He needed it. She heard the door slam behind him as Jake and Edwin began tidying up.

"I don't understand why he's so adamant Lars killed his wife. Lars is very stoic, but that doesn't mean he isn't grieving his wife."

"Who knows? You have to admit Mack has experience and good instincts, but he can be wrong, too," Jake said.

She was just going to say goodbye when the telephone rang shrilly inside the morgue. Edwin rushed to answer it.

"Not a good sign. I expect we're being called out," Jake said. "You should go home. I'd offer to take you, but I'm afraid that's a call to death."

Edwin rushed back. "A dead body on the street. In South Boston, 227 D Street. It's Mr. Callahan, the older one. And his daughter-in-law is with him."

Chapter Twenty-Eight

With the dinner over, and the awards handed out, Peter was finally able to sneak out to the club porch for a smoke. He didn't really like the cigars that were made available on a side table, but it was an excuse to escape his father's supercilious comments on policing. Peter started a discussion of a controversial racing rule that always irked his father, then left him and his companions debating it while he slipped away.

It was sharply cold outside, but the dining room had become hot and smoky after the meal, so Peter walked to the end of the porch, where he could see the empty docks. A boat with an engine had pulled up while they were eating. Three shadowy figures walked up the drive. He stepped back when he saw Sumner come out the door and down the stairs to meet the men.

There were lanterns hanging from the porch and as one of the men stepped into the light, Peter jerked to attention. Was that Mack? What was he doing here? He was wearing oilskins and boots, but Peter recognized the big frame, the big nose, and the short hair. He felt his blood rush to his head. What was going on? When Sumner stepped into the light beside the man, Peter saw him move and realized he was shorter than Mack and leaner. Also, he wore a mustache and sideburns, while Mack was clean-shaven. Not Mack. This must be one of the brothers. Peter had glimpsed them in a boat at the dock the day of the near accident, but he hadn't met them.

Taking care to stay in the shadows, Peter saw Sumner take a package from his coat and hand it to Mack's brother. He strained to hear.

"Those are the papers. She's a fine boat, certainly fast enough for your purposes," Sumner said. Peter heard some regret in his voice. Was he really selling or giving his prize racing boat to an Irish seaman? There didn't seem to be any money changing hands. What was Sumner getting for the boat?

"Don't worry. We'll be takin' good care of her," Mack's brother said. "And when you're sipping your cognac while others go thirsty, you'll be happy for it."

"And a share of the profit," Sumner said drily.

"Of course, of course, don't you worry. This'll be a profitable venture for all of us."

In the lamplight, Peter saw a grin that reminded him of Mack at his most annoying. So, Sumner was getting into the illegal liquor trade. Peter's father would be happy if the man was accused of it, but then Peter was sure his father would have his own sources. And, if he didn't, Peter was sure he'd buy from Sumner if he had to. Their animosity was confined to races round the buoys.

At that moment, three motorcars roared up the drive, shooting out gravel as they went. Mack's brother quickly melted into the shadows with his companions. Peter watched them head toward where *Eagle* was docked.

Sumner stood his ground, watching with disapproval as men jumped out of the cars and began searching among the other motorcars parked on the grass. "What's the meaning of this?" Sumner demanded.

When Peter saw it was his boss, Chief Detective McKenna, who climbed the steps, he was dumbfounded. He slid further into the darkness, not eager to be seen.

"We're looking for William Callahan Jr. He's here, isn't he?" McKenna growled at Sumner, who loomed over him. Peter stifled a groan. McKenna wasn't waiting till Monday. Peter felt anger rise up his neck, choking him. He knew it would be foolish to step forward, but he wanted to strangle his chief at that moment.

Before Peter had time to wonder why the rude McKenna didn't plunge into the club party to arrest Callahan, another detective, who was a stooge of McKenna's, rushed up.

"We found it!" He waved a rifle in the air. "In Callahan's motor, like we thought!"

"Come on." McKenna brushed past Sumner and stomped into the club. Peter joined the crowd of uniformed and plainclothes policemen who followed. Inside, the stocky McKenna in his bowler hat yelled Bill Callahan's name, and the crowd parted before him like Moses at the Red Sea. Bill looked startled as McKenna faced him, and he was surrounded by McKenna's men.

Waving the rifle, McKenna declared. "William Callahan, I'm arresting you for the murder of Ingrid Ericksson. Come with us."

His face burning, Peter watched as McKenna led Bill Callahan away in triumph. For the first time, he doubted his decision to become a policeman.

Chapter Twenty-Nine

"Did you say Eileen Callahan is there?" Fanny asked as Jake and Edwin prepared to go to the site of the death. She told them how Eileen had objected to her father-in-law's plan to go to South Boston. "I'll come along. Please. The poor woman, I feel so bad for her. I don't know why Mr. Callahan went to South Boston, but she must have been very worried about him to follow him there."

"Police told me there's no sign of trouble," Edwin said. "He dropped dead on the sidewalk. They think he was probably drunk."

Poor Mr. Callahan. He'd seemed so robust when she met him. It would be a terrible shock to the family. Perhaps he had a heart condition. Was that why he'd withdrawn from work? Fanny liked the young Eileen Callahan and didn't want her to face Jake and the police alone. Jake was used to dealing with the relatives of the dead, but the thought of the young woman out in the street with the body of her father-in-law was disturbing. Fanny refused to listen to Jake's advice to go home.

"All right, all right," Jake gave in. "Edwin, call the hospital people to bring an ambulance for the body. Mrs. Lee and I will go in *Suffolk Sue*."

Fanny almost regretted insisting on going when she climbed into Jake's old Model T. She knew it was Jake's pride and joy, but anyone else would balk at a ride in the old machine. Jake helped her into the second seat while Edwin opened a garage door and cranked the engine in the front. They rolled out onto the street, where Jake revved the engine, then started up with alarms clanging and lights flashing.

Fanny held on as they drove through the busy streets of Scollay Square

111

and over a bridge to the quieter streets of South Boston. It was cold as they whizzed by, mostly unlit windows of two- and three-decker homes. Fanny cringed at the noise and lights. They'd be waking people up, that was sure. They turned up D Street and lurched to a stop outside the brick front of a pub.

Jake directed one of *Suffolk Sue*'s spotlights at a crowd of people beside the building, and they all blinked and shaded their eyes as they turned to him. "Medical examiner," he shouted as he jumped down, leaving Fanny to climb down herself.

A uniformed policeman, looking worried, stepped forward. "He's here, Dr. Magrath. He collapsed. They wanted to move him, but I could see he was dead, and I kept them off." Fanny was sure Jake must have made an impression on the young patrolman in the past. She'd heard Jake shout loud recriminations at policemen who failed to follow his procedures. She thought it was a good thing he was teaching them to leave the body as it was found until the medical examiner arrived. He'd taught this one.

The crowd shifted, and she saw the older William Callahan lying face down on the brick pavement. His white hair was ruffled, and a top hat sat a foot away. His coat and scarf looked disheveled. Had he been so drunk he was wildly stumbling around with his coat undone? The image hardly matched the laconic man she'd met that afternoon. She wondered if he'd been thrown out of the pub that was several steps away. The aproned bartender, watching with a worried frown, looked vaguely familiar. Edwin had just arrived with the ambulance, and he clapped the bartender on the shoulder and led him away to talk to him.

Eileen Callahan squatted uselessly beside the dead man, white-faced but not weeping. Fanny saw her shudder slightly in the cold. An older woman, wearing a big overcoat but with slippers on her feet, stood by Eileen's shoulder. Who was she? Other neighbors and patrons of the bar hovered a few feet away, all shooed off by the patrolman.

Fanny hugged herself as she watched Jake examine the body. Old William Callahan had still seemed powerful when Fanny saw him that afternoon, but now he lay like a deflated balloon. Jake briefly felt his neck, looked at his hands and feet, examined the sidewalk, and, with Edwin's help, lifted the man enough to see his front. They murmured together, then set the body back down. Jake stood up with a grunt and looked at Eileen. "You're Mrs. Callahan?"

"Yes, this is my father-in-law. Apparently, he fell down. Was it his heart? He was getting on, and we tried to tell him to take it easy, but he wouldn't slow down." Tears gleamed in her eyes.

"You were here?" Jake put out a hand to help her up.

"I, no, no. I mean, I had come to look for him. I expected him home sooner." She glanced at Fanny and must have remembered that she was present when Callahan had announced his intention to go to South Boston that afternoon. "I was looking for him, and I found him…"

Jake glanced at Fanny. While he had plenty of experience at death scenes, she knew he wanted her to handle the shocked younger woman. Fanny stepped to Eileen's side and took her elbow. "I'm so sorry," she said.

Jake motioned to Edwin and the hospital men. They moved in to tip the body onto a stretcher. Fanny felt Eileen shift, getting weak-kneed at the sight. "Here, let's find a place for you to sit down," she said, guiding Eileen to a low wall. The woman shivered, and Fanny was afraid she'd collapse, but instead, she clutched Fanny's hand. "I must go home and tell Bill. He'll be home from Marblehead by now," she said, looking around. "I came in a cab. It should be waiting for me." She stumbled as she tried to rise but got her balance and waved over a man on the outskirts of the crowd. "Thank you, Mrs. Lee. Thank you so much. The cab will take me home now." She caught a sob before she could break down.

A sturdy middle-aged man offered his arm, her cab driver. Eileen leaned on him, stopping only for a word with Jake, who told her he would need to examine the body due to the suddenness of the death. Fanny thought Eileen would lose her composure at that, but she straightened up and said she would have her husband contact Jake in the morning.

The crowd dispersed as the body disappeared into the ambulance. Fanny saw the woman in slippers limp away. Most of the men headed back to the bar. Edwin helped Fanny back into *Suffolk Sue* as Jake turned off the spotlight. Edwin told them he knew the bartender. It turned out the man was the brother of Fanny's former housekeeper, Theresa, whom Edwin was courting. That explained why Fanny had thought he looked familiar.

"He said Mr. Callahan definitely didn't come from the pub," Edwin told them. "The bartender and the other men came out after he was found here."

Jake shook his head. "Where the devil *did* he come from then? And what was he doing down here anyway?"

Chapter Thirty

On Saturday morning, Jake found Edwin at the morgue. Jake wanted to know what had caused the elder Callahan to drop dead on a street in South Boston. Was it just a coincidence that he died when two murders were being investigated in his backyard in East Boston? It seemed unlikely.

Before they could retrieve the corpse from refrigeration, there was a hesitant knock on the door. Edwin went to answer and returned with Peter. The young detective had a canvas bag in his hands. He told them how Bill Callahan had been arrested the previous night.

"Mrs. Lee told me you planned to be in this morning. I have something for you. She said Bill's father is dead."

Jake told Peter how they'd found Bill's father in South Boston.

"Poor Eileen. Bill arrested, and Old Will dead, that's two blows. She must be devastated." Peter raised the bag. "I've got the gun that McKenna and his men found in Bill's Ford. I thought you'd want to test it."

"McKenna let you take it?" Jake was surprised. He didn't think Peter's superior believed in the latest advances in forensic technologies.

"Not exactly. I got it from the evidence locker. Bill claimed it wasn't his. What happened with the rifle from Lars and the one from Bill's father?"

"Neither one matched the bullet from the porch," Edwin spoke up. He took the rifle from Peter and looked at Jake.

"Yes. Test it," Jake said. Edwin headed for the garage.

"I couldn't believe it when McKenna showed up with his goons," Peter said. He was telling Jake about his evening at the yacht club when there was a loud banging at the door.

Jake rolled his eyes. It had to be Mack. He must have heard about Callahan's arrest and barged over from East Boston. Jake contemplated leaving the big Irishman out in the cold and pretending the morgue was empty on a Saturday.

"I'll go," Peter said.

He returned, trailed by a red-faced Mack, into the morgue examination room.

"What the hell is going on? You arrested Bill Callahan!" Mack shouted. He grabbed Peter by the shoulder. "Are you daft?"

Peter pulled away and turned to face him. "I didn't arrest him. McKenna did."

"You bleeding milksop. You let that nasty, drunken little weasel arrest Callahan. You gutless worm. It's your investigation, isn't it?"

"Mack. Stop." Jake said.

The big man turned toward him. "Stop! What'd ya mean, stop? He's ruining everything."

"Mack," Jake said, "They found another rifle in Bill's automobile. Edwin is testing it now." Jake reminded him that neither of the earlier guns matched the bullet from the porch.

Mack closed his eyes and swayed as he took in this information. Jake frowned at him. This wasn't looking good. Sure enough, the big man opened his eyes wide and turned on Peter again. "Testing. You're testing. But why in God's name would Bill Callahan have a rifle in his motorcar? You think he goes out nights shooting rabbits or something? Are you mad?" He glowered.

"No, of course not. I don't know," Peter said. "McKenna just showed up, and his men found the rifle in Bill's Ford. That's all I know."

"But *why* would he have a rifle, and *why* would he want to kill Ingrid? *Why, why, why?*" With each "why," Mack stepped closer to Peter, who moved back until he was hemmed in by one of the examination tables.

"Stop it, Mack," Jake said.

Peter put out a hand to push the big man back, and that began the fight. Mack raised a fist and slammed Peter in the face. He stepped back as Peter doubled over, but then the detective rammed his head into Mack's stomach, and they fell in a heap. Mack kicked him and slammed Peter to the ground, kneeling astride the younger man as he pummeled his head. Peter grabbed one of the big fists with both hands and tried to fend him off.

"Stop!" Jake yelled. Edwin rushed in from the garage. The two on the ground were still flailing and rolling. Edwin lifted a boot and kicked Mack in the face, which stopped him for a minute. Mack rolled onto his back, and Peter scrambled up, his nose streaming blood.

"What the hell," Peter grumbled.

When Mack made a move to get up, Edwin raised his boot again. The big man sat back on his elbows, heaving for breath.

Jake held a warning hand up to Mack on the floor. "Stop it, now. I don't understand, in fact, we all don't understand why you're so sure Bill Callahan didn't shoot Ingrid."

"He told me he wasn't even your friend," Peter mumbled around a handkerchief he held to his nose.

Mack was still catching his breath. "He had no reason," he said dejectedly.

Jake had enough. "I know you don't want to believe it. But how can you be so sure Ingrid wasn't having an affair with Bill Callahan?"

Sweat poured down Mack's face as he looked up. "Because I was. I was the one she was seeing."

Chapter Thirty-One

"Why didn't you say so?" Peter asked.

They had lifted Mack onto a hard wooden chair, and he was bent over, his shoulders heaving as he wept. Edwin shook his head in disgust and left to go back to his test in the garage. Jake pulled up another chair for himself while Peter tilted his head back, still trying to stop the nosebleed. He leaned against one of the tables.

Mack sat up, breathing heavily. "We were two lost souls. We took comfort. That Lars is a cold one, and Ingrid was more warm and lively like. But he brought her down. She was down, and I was down. About the job, about Mary...my girl left me when I lost my job. Ingrid saw I was drinkin' myself sick from it, and she came to me and took the bottle away and replaced it with her lips." He wiped away tears with a big paw and a loud sniffle. "It wasn't like she'd ever leave that big oaf or little Lilly. I was sure Lars had found out and got his cold vengeance. He'd be one to do it."

"There's no evidence of that, Mack," Jake told him. "We're sure it wasn't his rifle used to shoot her. But why didn't you tell us?"

Peter wagged his head, agreeing with Jake. He kept the handkerchief pressed as he watched with one eye, head tipped back.

Mack's face scrunched up. "Aww, it was wrong. We knew it. We'd no desire to hurt anyone, even that Lars. Though he did whack her if she was late with his dinner." He was making excuses, but Jake could tell he was coming to realize that Lars might not be the one who had killed Ingrid. "My sister Kate'd skin me alive if she found out. So, we were careful. Poor Ingrid. Who'd do such a thing to a pretty little mite like her? Bill had no reason. He's wild for Eileen in any case. No matter, she's a real Amazon."

The big Irishman was attracted to the softer Ingrid. But how did he know Bill wasn't also seduced by the young woman? Peter exchanged a glance with Jake. They were both getting a different view of Ingrid, who had kept her liaison with Mack so secret. What other secrets did she have? Peter was sure neither one of them believed Mack would have killed the woman just to keep his sister from finding out. And, if Lars found out, Mack would be happy to go head-to-head with the big Swede. Peter shuddered to think what such a confrontation would look like.

Peter squeezed his nose and spoke around his bloody handkerchief. "Where did the gun come from? The one in Bill's car?" He gulped. "That's why they arrested him."

Mack wiped his eyes with big hands. "It's not him, I tell you. Bill probably wouldn't know how to fire the damn rifle. It was his brother in the navy who did some hunting or his father. Not Bill. I tell you, I don't believe there was a rifle in that car." He banged a fist on his knee.

"You think they put it there to frame him?" Jake asked.

Peter tried to shake his head no but had to tip it up again to stop the nosebleed. Jake agreed. "Look, we know McKenna is incompetent," Jake said. "But you can't believe he put the rifle in Bill's motorcar. That would be a crime." Peter wondered. He wasn't sure they could assume McKenna wouldn't put the gun in Bill Callahan's automobile. McKenna wanted to arrest the man, no matter what.

"He's a clown," Mack insisted. "He and his goons do whatever they want."

Making a huge effort, Peter unclasped his nose and said, "But where did he get it? Whose gun was it?"

At that moment, Edwin came in from the garage. He bit his lip as he looked at Mack. The big Irishman could have been a lion let loose from his cage and barely controlled by his trainer. With one eye on Mack, Edwin said, "That's it. The rifle they found in Bill Callahan's motorcar matches the bullet that killed Ingrid Ericksson."

119

Chapter Thirty-Two

When Fanny arrived at the morgue, she saw Peter leading Mack away. Inside, Jake and Edwin were about to begin the autopsy on William Callahan senior.

"Was that Peter and Mack I saw leaving?" she asked. She hung her coat on a wall hook and took out her notepad and pencil before pulling up a stool. Jake and Edwin exchanged a glance.

Jake told her how Peter and Mack had come to blows. "They looked friendly enough when they walked away." They'd had their backs to her, too far away to greet.

"It cleared the air some," Jake told her as Edwin folded back the sheet on poor Old Will.

"What were they fighting about?"

"Bill Callahan was arrested last night. Not by Peter, but by McKenna. The police showed up at the yacht club, found a rifle in Callahan's automobile, and arrested him. Mack was furious."

"What a mess," Fanny said. "Poor Eileen. Her father-in-law dead, and her husband arrested. She must be terribly upset." When Fanny left South Boston the night before, she'd known from Edwin's test that the senior Callahan's rifle didn't shoot Ingrid. She thought Bill Callahan must be in the clear. But he'd been arrested.

"Is it true that Bill and Ingrid were seeing each other secretly, then?" Fanny asked.

Jake coughed. He looked at the chair standing out of place in the middle of the room. Fanny was puzzled. Before she could ask, he told her. "It seems that Mrs. Ericksson was seeing someone else. Not Bill Callahan."

"Who?" Fanny asked. It annoyed her how men always wanted to protect women from knowing about an affair. As if they couldn't deal with sordid details. She was disappointed in Jake. Why couldn't he just tell her?

He sighed. "Mack."

"Mack?" Fanny was astonished. Somehow, she couldn't picture the big Irishman with the small Swedish woman. He was so gruff. She'd never have imagined him with romantic feelings. But, of course, that was her own ignorance. She had to rid herself of her assumptions that everyone acted like the people she grew up with in the rarefied air of the upper classes. She disliked Mack. But it pained her to think how he must have felt to see his lover on Jake's examination table. "Why didn't he tell you before this?"

"He didn't want to blacken her memory, and he was sure her husband had found out and killed her. That's why he was so intent on accusing Lars."

"Mack should have told you from the start that he was the one seeing Ingrid." Fanny found it hard to forgive the ex-detective. He should have known better. "He kept insisting the dead woman wouldn't have betrayed her husband. Honestly." Fanny shook her head. "Well, Mack's sister did say Ingrid was a bit of a flirt." She wondered if Kate had known about the relationship between her brother and the dead woman. "What will happen now? Doesn't this mean there's no motive for Bill Callahan? Will they let him go?"

"I doubt it. Even if Mack came out with his story, and we're not sure he should, McKenna has the gun. And Edwin matched it to the bullet that killed Ingrid Ericksson."

"Oh, no," Fanny said. She'd assumed this wonderful new process for matching bullets to guns had cleared Eileen's husband, but now it would prove him guilty.

"Bill had the opportunity," Jake said. "He could have left his office that day to shoot her, then gone back. We decided to wait and see what motive McKenna comes up with. There's Leary's death, too. Presumably, McKenna will try to get Bill for that death as well. We want to hear what the police say about that.

"Peter's not fond of his superior, so he agreed not to tell McKenna what Mack told us. If they bring Bill to trial, Mack could testify for Bill's defense that he was the one having a relationship with Ingrid."

"But how did the gun that shot Ingrid get into Bill's car?" Fanny asked. Now that she knew about Mack's liaison with Ingrid, she was as sure as Mack was that Bill Callahan had no reason to kill her.

Jake shrugged. Edwin said, "Detective Attwood thinks someone planted the rifle in Mr. Callahan's motor to frame him for the murder."

"But who?' Fanny asked. "Not the police, surely?"

Jake shook his head. "Chief Detective McKenna was hellbent on arresting Bill Callahan, but even he wouldn't plant the gun. Besides, where would he get it?'

"Poor Eileen," Fanny groaned. "She must be reeling from all of this. Can't you at least let her know that Mack, not Bill, was Ingrid's lover?"

Jake frowned at Fanny's blunt description. "I don't think so. She might spill it all to the police or the press. It'll be better for Bill if we keep that secret hidden till it's needed." He turned back to the table. "In any case, we need to see what happened to Will here."

Fanny took notes as Jake recited the name and circumstances of where they had found the dead man. He commented on the state of the head, hands, and feet, then Edwin helped remove the clothes to pile them on another table. When they got to the fine linen shirt, they tipped the man up to almost sitting.

"Now, what is this?" Jake said to himself. "Look at that." Jake pointed to a band of purplish color on the man's back. "That's lividity."

By now, Fanny was used to viewing dead bodies. She was determined to learn as much as she could about the work, taking notes and drawing sketches as needed. She remembered earlier lessons. "He was lying on his back after he died," she said.

"But we found him..." Jake prompted.

"Lying on his face, on the sidewalk." Fanny vividly remembered the scene, Eileen hunched over the body, William on his stomach.

Jake and Edwin scrutinized the purple blotches. "The depth of the lividity indicates he was on his back for some time after he died."

"Then someone turned him over?" Fanny asked.

"Or moved him."

"But who?"

"That's what I'd like to know." Jake proceeded to turn the body face up, and he used a scalpel to do a complete autopsy, removing and weighing organs. Fanny took scrupulous notes and Edwin helped move specimens to jars. After an hour, Jake sewed up the open chest. He slid the sheet back over the corpse. "There's no question he died of a heart attack. There are no signs of struggle, no wounds, and no signs of poison in his system. There are all the signs of a massive heart attack. But he didn't drop down dead on the sidewalk, like we thought."

"Then, what happened?" Fanny asked.

"He was moved after he died," Jake told her, and Edwin nodded in agreement.

"But if he died naturally, as you said, why would someone move him?" Fanny asked.

Jake thought about that as he moved some instruments to the sink where Edwin was cleaning up.

"That's a very good question," he said. "There are a number of questions I'd like to ask Eileen Callahan. How did she get there so fast, anyhow? She just happened to be driving down the street in a part of town where she doesn't live and has no business, and she finds her father-in-law dead on the street? It doesn't ring true, does it?"

Fanny shook her head. It didn't. "But why would Eileen lie? Jake, you can't tell the police that. Poor Eileen has enough trouble with her husband arrested for murder. You can't get her suspected by the police, too. They have two young children, and she'll have to see to her dead father-in-law's funeral. It's too much."

Jake frowned. "Why don't you go over and talk to her before I tell anyone about this. I have a suspicion. If I'm right, she's more likely to tell you the truth than me." Jake looked puzzled. "It's definitely a natural death, but why was he moved? What was he doing in South Boston anyhow? Is there some connection there? I don't understand. It seems to me there's more to these deaths in East Boston than simple jealousy."

Fanny gathered her bag. "If you think she'll talk to me, I'll go to her. Poor woman, I'm sure she'll need support. I'll find out what I can. I promise."

"Tell her that if she gives you an explanation, I'll be able to release the body for burial. Tell her I must have an explanation before I can give a death certificate."

Fanny wondered if Jake already knew what that explanation would be as she hurried off to find a taxicab.

Chapter Thirty-Three

In East Boston, Fanny found a distraught Eileen in her husband's office in the house on Meridian Street. Kate Gallagher stood over her. She looked up when a young maid brought Fanny in.

"Mrs. Lee, have you heard? They arrested my husband."

"Yes, I'm so sorry."

"Bill would never hurt anyone. Certainly not Ingrid." Eileen was near tears.

"Unfortunately, they found a rifle in his automobile, and the police believe it's the gun used to shoot Mrs. Ericksson."

"No." Eileen had stood up, but now she dropped back into her husband's chair behind the desk. "A gun. No, no, no. Bill doesn't have a gun." She waved her hands over the papers spread out on the desk. "What am I going to do? There's a big meeting next week about a new tunnel. Bill was all excited about the contract. And now his father is dead, and he doesn't even know it. I don't know what to do."

Kate moved around the desk to put a hand on her shoulder. "What about Old Will?" she asked Fanny. "We'll need to get the funeral home to prepare him, then hold the wake here."

Eileen gulped a breath to stop a sob. She stared at Fanny wide-eyed.

"I've come from the mortuary. Dr. Magrath has determined that your father-in-law died of a heart attack."

"Well, at least there's no question of murder there," Kate said. Eileen swallowed.

"But there's one question Dr. Magrath needs answered before he can release the body," Fanny said. "It's clear from the body that Mr. Callahan died on his back, but he was moved after he died. How did he end up face down on the ground, Eileen?" Fanny hated to be rough with the young woman, but she thought she needed to shock her into telling the truth. "You know, don't you?"

Eileen hid her face in her hands and hunched her shoulders.

Kate patted her back. "Please, Mrs. Lee, can't they just release the poor man. Look what Eileen has had to go through."

Fanny shook her head. "Dr. Magrath needs to know what happened. He can keep it confidential if that's what you're worried about. But you have to tell the truth."

Kate took a big breath. "You need to tell them." She looked at Eileen. "It's of no matter now, you know."

Eileen looked up at her with alarm.

"Of course, we knew. Everybody in the neighborhood knew." Kate told Eileen. "We've known Old Will since forever. No one minded, you know. He's been a widower for years now. Tell Mrs. Lee."

Eileen put her hands flat on the table. She shivered slightly as she looked up at Fanny. "My father-in-law was visiting a...a lady in South Boston. She telephoned me last night. He collapsed at her house." She sighed. "In her bed, you see."

"So, you went over and moved him to the street so people wouldn't know?" Fanny asked. She sympathized. Eileen would be disgraced if people knew the old man had died in the bed of his mistress.

"It was horrid," Eileen said. "I sent the driver away to return in an hour. We got Pa dressed. It took both of us." She shivered. "We rolled him off the bed and onto a rug, and then we got him down the stairs and into the street. It was as far as we could carry him, just the two of us."

Fanny imagined it must have been a nightmare for the young wife, dressing the dead body, then dragging it outside. All to hide the circumstances of the death. Fanny remembered the older woman who stood near the body in coat and slippers. It must have been her house beside the pub.

"Oh, please. People can't know. He'd be a laughingstock," Eileen moaned.

"Poor Bill. How can I tell him about this?"

"There's no reason at all for anyone to know, is there?" Kate asked. She bristled ferociously at Fanny, daring her to dispute the situation. Her maternal instincts to shield her friend were strong. "We all knew he had a lady friend, but Eileen is right. It would make him a dirty joke if they knew he died in her bed."

"I think Dr. Magrath will understand," Fanny told them. "Is there a telephone I could use to tell him?"

When Fanny returned from the telephone, she was able to tell them that the body could be picked up by the funeral home people that day. Dr. Magrath also advised that Eileen hire a criminal lawyer for her husband.

"Jerry McDowell," Eileen said.

"Aye, he's got the connections for sure," Kate told her. "And you should call Honey Fitz and the others in his party; they'll help him."

Eileen pulled out a leather-bound address book and began to write down names and numbers. Kate ushered Fanny out.

Chapter Thirty-Four

Fanny wanted to see Lars Ericksson before she returned to Beacon Hill, so she followed Kate back to the three-decker. They exited the front door on Meridian Street, then took an alley to the back and climbed stairs down the hill. She could see the backs of the warehouses on Border Street below, with the docks and inner harbor beyond.

When they reached the back door of the three-decker, Kate said, "They're thinking Bill was seeing Ingrid, aren't they?"

Jake had warned Fanny not to tell anyone about Mack's relationship with the dead woman. She wondered if Kate already knew about her brother's romance. "I don't know, but I think they'll see that as a motive," she said.

Kate frowned. "It wasn't him. Ingrid had a way with men. She tried flirting with Bill, with his father, too." Kate bit her lip, standing still in the yard. "Aw, that Mack! How many times have I told him to get himself together? He's such a big baby these days. Wait till I get my hands on him."

She flung open the door and stamped up the steps to where one of her brothers was watching her children. Based on what Kate had just said, Fanny was sure now that she knew about her brother Mack's relationship with Ingrid. But Kate obviously felt she couldn't admit it to an outsider. Mack would get an earful from his sister, and Fanny thought he deserved it.

She continued to the third floor, where she knocked. After a wait, Lars opened the door. He looked shabby, in worn clothes and socks on his feet. The little girl Lilly was nowhere to be seen, so Fanny assumed she was downstairs with Kate's children.

Inside, she saw the manager of the Sumner company, Ian Stewart, chomping on his pipe as he sat by a chess set on the kitchen table. He stood at her arrival. She nodded a greeting.

"Mr. Ericksson, I don't know if you've heard, but the elder Mr. Callahan died last night. And the younger Mr. Callahan has been arrested for your wife's murder."

The big Swede looked stunned. "Will? Old Will is dead? How?"

"Oh my," Ian said, taking the pipe from his mouth.

"He had a heart attack. He was found on a street in South Boston," Fanny told them.

"I'm sorry to hear it," Ian said. "What a tragedy. I hope he wasn't over there to see that Gustin Gang. There's some who believe they're behind the sabotage at the works. They're dangerous." He looked grim. "You came to tell Lars Old Will is dead? That's good of you. They were very close." Fanny thought the little man was speaking on behalf of the silent Lars.

"I also wanted to consult him about a couple of other things," Fanny said. She didn't want to advertise her business to the Sumner man, and she thought perhaps she should leave and return another time. But Ian Stewart politely grabbed his hat and said his goodbyes. The whiff of pipe smoke followed him out.

Lars looked like he was sleepwalking as he went to the table where the chessboard was set out and sat down. Fanny followed him in, closing the door behind her.

"I'm so sorry. I know you were friends with Mr. Callahan. It was a shock to his family." She sat down opposite him.

He stared at her. "They arrest Bill?"

"Yes."

"He killed Ingrid. Old Will died of shame. He killed him, too."

Fanny knew Lars believed Bill was guilty of killing his wife. Now, he'd jumped to the conclusion that Bill had also caused his father's death. "You mustn't think that. I spoke to the older Mr. Callahan yesterday. He didn't believe his son killed your wife. And he died before he learned Bill was arrested. Mr. Ericksson, I don't believe Bill killed Ingrid, and neither do Detective Attwood and Dr. Magrath. His wife is sure that Bill didn't have any relationship with your wife, and I believe her." She couldn't tell Lars about Mack's revelation. It would only make things worse.

Lars stared at her. Then he made a fist and brought it down on the table, so the chess pieces jumped. Fanny sat back, away from him. Would he threaten her? He stood up. She shrank in her chair, stiff with anticipation, but he turned away to a cupboard where he took out a white linen handkerchief. He placed it on the table in front of her. She saw the initials "WHC" embroidered on the corner in silver thread.

"It was his. I found it in her drawer," Lars said. "Bill Callahan." He sat down heavily.

Fanny put out her hand and felt the smooth silk of the thread. "You think Bill gave this to her?"

He leaned on an elbow and put his forehead in his big hand.

Fanny wasn't sure what to say to him. She dropped the handkerchief on the table and pushed it away. "Perhaps you should give it to Detective Attwood and tell him what you believe." Fanny remembered what Kate had said about Ingrid flirting. Could she have been seeing both men? The thought repulsed her. And yet, now the dead woman would never be able to defend her reputation. Fanny stood up.

"I wonder if you've completed the work I asked for?" There was nothing she could do about the handkerchief, but she could help find the truth about the woman's death.

He stood. "Yes, yes. I can get it for you."

Fanny had commissioned the carpenter on her previous trip. She'd given very precise instructions. She'd kept it secret from Jake and the others, wanting to see the result before she shared her idea. She wasn't sure if they'd find this as useful as she thought it could be.

Lars went out the kitchen door to the balcony, returning with a large box. He set it on the floor, removed the chess set from the table, opened the box, and lifted out a doll's house.

"Yes," Fanny said as he placed it on the table. "It's just what I wanted. Let me look."

Chapter Thirty-Five

On Monday, Jake found Fanny and Peter at the morgue. Quite the early birds. Edwin had let them in. Now, he helped Peter carry in a large box. They set it on the floor of the empty garage bay where they'd tested the guns. It was three feet wide and four feet high. Jake was suspicious. Had they found more evidence?

He could see that Edwin was uneasy, not sure if his boss would approve, but the young man couldn't deny Fanny's request to bring the box in. And Peter. Fanny must have bullied him to help her get the box to the morgue. The young detective didn't seem as excited as Fanny about the whole undertaking. But he, too, wasn't able to rebel against her demands. Jake frowned. She might push around the younger men, but he wouldn't stand for it. "What's going on?" he asked.

"You'll see. Lift it out, please, and put it on the table," Fanny said. Her face was slightly pink with suppressed excitement.

When they set the item on the table and removed a covering tarp, Jake saw it was a skillful, if rough, reproduction of the house and backyard where Ingrid was killed. It was the size of a dollhouse, made of thin wood, with one side open. The rear of the toy three-decker had three porches with roughhewn little railings. It reminded Jake of gingerbread houses in his childhood.

Fanny opened her carpetbag and brought out her sketchpad. She began adding small pieces of furniture to the scene as she looked at her drawings. Made from boxes, the furniture was crude, but she was careful to place a little chair on the third-floor porch, where Ingrid would have stood to hang laundry.

Jake remembered how Franny had created a miniature room the previous winter, and it had helped a witness remember telling details about a death. She was trying to do it again. Jake went to his office to hang up his coat and returned with an extra chair to watch the proceedings.

Fanny carefully hung little strings with tiny towels and pieces of clothing from the rafters of the second and third-floor porches. Ingrid and Kate both had laundry hanging when Ingrid fell to her death. Fanny swung the hammock and placed the couch used by Mack and his brother on the bottom floor. Her attention to detail was scrupulous. The porch railing on the top floor was pulled away on the corner, and a tiny flowerbox that hung on the second-floor railing was also partly falling off. Fanny consulted her sketches from the first day they had visited. She looked dissatisfied.

"There hasn't been enough time to get dollhouse furniture. I had to make do with cutting up small boxes, but you can get the idea," she said. Jake knew she had created a miniature of the full Chicago Symphony Orchestra for her parents. It had been a marvel. She obviously didn't think this creation was as good.

Franny placed one little doll leaning over the second-floor porch, Kate Gallagher. The young mother had rushed out from her kitchen after Ingrid fell. She placed another doll face down on the ground below. Ingrid Ericksson. Jake could see the dolls were handmade, complete with tiny details of the clothing. Fanny had been busy.

The model house was open on the side, so Jake could see inside the kitchens. Fanny put a tall male doll on a chair in the top-floor kitchen, Lars Ericksson. Edwin and Peter stared at the little house.

"Skillfully done," Jake commented. "Did you make it?"

"I asked Mr. Ericksson to build it for me. He's a carpenter, after all. It's rough, but it's the best we could do so quickly." She frowned.

"Fanny, he's a suspect in the death of his wife. You shouldn't be visiting him." Jake was alarmed sometimes at the lengths to which she would go to try to impress him. Not just to impress. She was determined to find a way to help with the death investigations. It would be useless to try to forbid her to do anything once she got it into her head. Mack and Peter could go out and interrogate people. Edwin had his laboratory to contribute scientific results in the hunt for the truth. But Fanny was constrained by her sex, her age, and her social position. Creating the miniature of the scene was her way of participating in the investigation. Apparently, her notes and drawings weren't enough to satisfy her.

"But we know Lars Ericksson's rifle didn't kill his wife," she protested. "I don't see a problem with asking him to build a model of the house."

"We may *believe* he didn't kill his wife based on the comparison of the bullet from his rifle and the one that killed her. But I'm not sure a court would allow the bullet evidence. It's new science. We may be ahead of them in our thinking. It can take a while for the judicial system to accept new ideas." Jake wanted to encourage Edwin in his growing interest in the scientific advances that would help investigations, but he had to warn them all that it would take time to convince the courts to accept this type of evidence.

"Yes, but look, Jake." Fanny took the doll Ingrid and stood her on the little chair on the third-floor porch, as if she were hanging laundry. "See? If she was standing here, the shot couldn't have come from inside the kitchen. That's where Lars was. It had to come from outside, probably below. Do you see it?"

Jake shook his head, not as a negative answer to her question, but as a sign of frustration. Fanny had decided Lars did not kill his wife, so she was content to have him build her model house. He was afraid that even if she thought he had done it, she was so single-minded that she'd still use his carpentry skills to build her a house. He wondered if he was doing the right thing in allowing her to participate in these investigations. He thought she was terribly naïve. But he wouldn't know how to stop her once she got something into her head. He shrugged.

"There was no one outside," Peter said. "Kate Gallagher came out immediately after Ingrid fell. Ingrid couldn't have been shot by someone in the yard because there was no one there."

"We don't know that she was standing on the chair," Edwin pointed out. What if she was leaning over the railing or the laundry basket? Could someone have shot her from above?"

Fanny frowned.

"What about from the first floor?" Jake asked. "Could one of the men down there have fired up and hit her?" Mack's brothers were an unknown quantity. To Jake, it seemed much more likely that one of them would have a gun and shoot it. Not aiming at Ingrid Ericksson, of course, but in some other dispute or drunken brawl. "Were the McNally brothers' home?" he asked Peter.

Peter consulted his notes. "Some of them. Sleeping from what they reported. Mack wasn't there; he was over here at a committee meeting. There were lots of people at that meeting who could vouch for him."

Jake looked at the young detective. Had he checked on Mack's alibi yet? Peter seemed reluctant to suspect the ex-detective, despite their fight. The big man's breakdown had made them all uncomfortable. But as the lover of the dead woman, he had a motive. Clearly, Peter didn't believe Mack could have killed her.

Edwin had another suggestion. "What about from the roof of the Callahan warehouse?" He used his hands to block a building and point at the roof. "Or from the side of the building, here?"

"There's that big iron thing at the side," Fanny said, consulting her sketchpad. "What is that?"

"It's an iron railway bridge that was dismantled. They kept it to use again somewhere or to take parts of it," Peter informed them.

"What about the other building across from that?" Edwin asked. "Maybe the shot came from there."

Fanny turned a page and showed them another sketch. "That's Sumner's office, warehouse, whatever. But it's blocked by the Callahan building, see? The shot couldn't have come from there."

Jake moved closer to examine the model house. "It still seems most likely that the shot was from the ground in front of the porches." He pointed to the spot where the dead body was found.

The doorbell rang.

"That must be the funeral home people for Mr. Callahan's body," Edwin said as he left to answer it.

Jake sighed. The Callahans had troubles, and now they'd have to bury the old man in the midst of the accusations that his son had killed his lover. Eileen would have to hold it together. He wondered if Bill Callahan had sufficient political pull to get out on bail in time for his father's funeral. And wake. The wake was even more important in these Irish American families.

Chapter Thirty-Six

On Wednesday evening, Peter was glad to hear that Bill Callahan had been released on bail in time for his father's wake. Jake refused to go, saying it was inappropriate for him, but Peter agreed to accompany Mrs. Lee. At Meridian Street, they followed a crowd of people and waited in line to greet Eileen Callahan and her husband in the parlor.

Old Will was laid out in an open casket at the back of the room, surrounded by flowers. People would pass through a reception line, saying a few words to the family, then they would step to the casket and the padded kneeler beside it to view the corpse and say a quick prayer. Peter watched as mourners, including Mack, greeted the young couple and then knelt by the dead man to say a prayer.

"I guess it's the custom," Peter whispered to Fanny. He hadn't attended this type of wake before. In his family's Protestant tradition, funerals concentrated on the church service and graveyard prayers.

Peter saw Ian Stewart follow his boss, Sumner, in the line ahead. They greeted the Callahans, then moved away, awkwardly avoiding the kneeler. They headed out immediately, not staying as other people were. On his way out, Ian stopped to say hello to Peter, who was still in line. "Barbaric custom, don't you think?" he said very quietly. Peter assumed he meant viewing the dead person in his own parlor. Ian cocked an eyebrow at Bill. "I see he got out. No doubt some of the Dem pols owe him. They'll all be along to pay homage. Bill and Old Will are big contributors."

Fanny seemed offended by the comments of the Scottish man. She ignored him pointedly as Peter said a hasty goodbye.

When they reached Eileen, Peter could see she was white with shock. Having Old Will's body in front of her and greeting all of the people who knew him must increase the feelings of loss for her. Peter recalled people trying to console him when his mother died, but their presence only made him feel the pain of her absence more deeply.

Eileen bent close to Fanny. Peter strained to hear. "Thank you so much for getting Pa released. I don't know what we would have done if they'd raised questions about his passing." She gulped. "And thank you for being discreet." She looked worried as her eyes traveled around the room.

"Certainly, and don't worry. Dr. Magrath and I would never betray your confidence." Peter could barely hear the exchange. Mrs. Lee squeezed Eileen's hand and stepped back to move on to her husband, Bill.

"Thank you for your help, Mrs. Lee," he said. He gave Peter a stiff nod. He looked worn, shifting his weight from foot to foot as if he had trouble standing still.

"I'm so sorry for your loss," she said, then she moved away, avoiding the kneeler. Muttering words of sympathy, Peter saw that the chairs lining the room were filled mostly by women, with a few men standing and talking. Feeling it would be rude to rush away, as Sumner had, Peter followed Mrs. Lee to a chair against the wall.

"We'll miss Old Will," the lady beside her said, and Fanny agreed. She started a conversation with the woman who said she was an old family friend, ignoring Peter, who had trailed after her.

Peter stood awkwardly a few feet away from Fanny's chair. He felt distinctly uncomfortable. He had been dunked into an environment that was completely foreign to him. He wanted to swim to the surface to get a breath, but he knew it would be rude to leave, and he was obliged to take Fanny home at the end of the night.

He looked around for Mack. He'd seen the big Irishman earlier on the kneeler. Peter had watched as Mack made a sign of the cross, like a secret signal of a mysterious cult. Where had he gone? Itchy for something to do, Peter was about to approach one of the old men standing around to ask about Mack when he heard a hiss and turned to see the ex-detective beckoning to him. He seemed to have come from a room at the back of the house and stuck his head into the parlor, looking for Peter.

Relieved, Peter walked to him, and Mack grabbed his arm and pulled him into a back room, then out onto a back porch. Peter had left his coat in the front room, where all the guests had piled their coats on chairs left out for that purpose, so he was freezing on the porch. "What are you doing?" he demanded.

Mack looked back and grinned. He stepped across the back porch, through an opening. Peter realized they must be crossing to the adjoining house where Bill and Eileen Callahan lived. He followed Mack through a door and into a parlor that mirrored the one where Old Will's body was laid out in the next building. This room was filled with smoke and noise. Couches and armchairs were supplemented with hard dining room chairs all filled by men smoking cigars or cigarettes and passing around a brown paper bag hiding a bottle. The cozy attitude and bursts of laughter contrasted with the murmured condolences in the room he'd left. He was shocked. How could they be so disrespectful? He was deeply offended on behalf of poor Eileen and her husband. He felt heat rising up his throat and to his face. Someone needed to say something.

Before he could step forward, Bill Callahan brushed past him, greeting Mack as he went by. Peter relaxed, thinking Bill would put these men in their place and throw them out, but instead, he stepped over to the man who had the bottle in the brown bag, took it from him, and took a large gulp.

Outraged, Peter started to move into the room, but Mack grabbed him by the back of his jacket and pulled him into the back room. "What do you think you're doing?" he hissed.

Peter was indignant. "Are you going to let them act like that? Drinking, laughing..." There was a shout of laughter from the other room. Peter hunched up ready to plunge back in, but Mack clutched the back of his collar, turned him around, and pushed him out into the night air. He shut the door behind them.

"You're makin' a fool of yourself," Mack hissed.

Peter shook loose from the big hand and straightened his jacket and tie. His face was hot despite the chill in the air. "I can't believe you're so disrespectful." He glared at Mack, whose forehead wrinkled with confusion.

"Here, now. What's going on?" Kate climbed the outside steps from the kitchen below, carrying a tray of small biscuits.

Mack stepped back to make room. "He's daft. He was going to make a scene in there." He nodded toward the room with the men. They heard another bout of men's laughter. Peter waited for Kate to go in and tell the men off.

But she handed her tray to Mack. "Here, you bring these in to the women. I'll take care of this." She wiped her hands on her apron as Mack grumbled, but he took his orders and left with the tray. "I see you've not been to an Irish wake before, have you, Detective Attwood?"

"No." Peter glanced at the door to the room where the men were. Why wasn't she making them stop? He could hear someone telling a story as the others listened. He couldn't make out the words.

"You know, I've sometimes helped with the food at Beacon Hill funerals. Well, the time they have after they've all been to the church and the graveyard. It's a sorry kind of party, I've always thought. They say hello to the widow or whoever's mourning, then sip some watery sherry while they stand around speaking in whispers. I've heard them mostly gossiping about the will and who gets the inheritance, like. Hardly a word to say about the dead man himself. It's like they avoid mentioning the poor soul."

Peter remembered his grandfather's funeral. The cold, austere Park Street Church. The ride to the graveyard where the preacher said prayers before they lowered the casket. The ride back to Louisburg Square and the hushed atmosphere as all the people in black or with black armbands stood around awkwardly. It had been draining. And the servants strung black bunting on the door and windows. The quiet and whispering had lasted for weeks.

Kate was watching him. "It's not our way at all," she said. "Now, what they're doing in there is telling stories about Old Will. They'll be remembering the funniest, most embarrassing, wittiest, and best days of his life. They'll each of them take a draft, then tell their best memory, then pass the bottle to the next man to do the same." She looked directly into Peter's eyes, and he felt a chilly wind whip him from behind. "You're thinkin' it's disrespectful, aren't you? But it's not. It's just they're burnishing his memory. By the time we go, we're most of us like a dirty penny, been stepped on and kicked around. But in there, they're rubbin' that penny, so it shines, polishing the good times so they stand out. And they'll all go away with a bright picture of Old Will and be talking of him for weeks now."

Mack came back. "They'll be starting the rosary," he told them.

Kate grinned. "So, there you go, Detective. You can go back in there with the women and listen to them say a novena, or you can go in with the men and hear stories with laughter and tears. I know where Mack will be goin'." She patted her brother on the arm. "But I need to get back down in the kitchen. If you think this is a big thing, you should come back after the funeral tomorrow, there'll be a feast and more stories." She slipped by Mack and hurried back to the kitchen.

Mack frowned at Peter. "Will you come in? But you must behave yourself. You can't..."

Peter put up a hand. "Okay. I get it. I'll be good. I promise."

The men quietly entered the parlor full of men. Honey Fitz, the former mayor of Boston, was telling a funny story about Will. Peter counted a half dozen prominent city politicians, including Jimmy Curley, another former mayor. The smoke of the room stung his eyes to tears, but he laughed with the rest of the men.

Chapter Thirty-Seven

The heat and smoke in the room suffocated Peter. He felt his eyes water, whether from laughter or smoke, he couldn't say. There was a lot of mock argument as men questioned the veracity of a taleteller before handing on the bottle. Each man learned more about the dead Will from someone else's story than they'd ever known during his life. Each anecdote filled in a different view of the dead man. All the brushstrokes were coming together to paint a sharper picture of Old Will Callahan.

Peter backed away to step out onto the porch for some air. It was steely cold but clear there. It woke him right up. Turning, he saw light and smoke billowing across the road at the docks below him. Fire! He opened the back door and called Mack.

The big Irishman rushed out and squinted. "That's the *Eagle*," he said, pointing to the docks. "I think there's someone on it,"

Peter recognized the boat that had belonged to Sumner. He hadn't told Mack about seeing his brother Sean do a deal with the Brahmin at the yacht club. The big main sail was partly down and shook back and forth, fanning the licks of flame from the deck. Two figures danced on the dock in the flickering light while another lay still on the deck, highlighted by the flames.

"Jesus," Mack said. "Fire!" he yelled to the men inside. Then he hopped down the back stairs connecting the porches. "Kate, for the love of God, call Joe and the fire trucks," he screamed as he passed the kitchen floor. Peter followed.

They raced across the yard and street and down to the docks. They reached a pile of crates and two men throwing buckets of water at the deck of the sailboat.

"It's Sean, Mack. We can't get to him," one of the men yelled as Mack reached the side where the boat drifted away. The boat was still on fire. Peter heard pounding beside him as Bill Callahan ran by to leap onto the flaming deck without stopping. By the time Mack pulled in the bow line, Bill had hoisted the unconscious man to his shoulder. With a big effort, he threw the body across to Mack and Peter, who dragged Sean away from the burning boat.

Clangs and whistles and the clip-clop of horses' hooves announced the arrival of the firetruck. Men in helmets carrying axes backed the machine down the dock. They started spraying a hose of water at the flames that licked up the mast of the big boat. One of them rushed down to the men on the dock.

"What's this?" a fireman asked, thumping a crate. Peter could see he was glancing around, estimating how the fire would spread.

"Ah, ah, it's whiskey. Perfectly legal," said one of the men who had been on the dock when they arrived. Peter assumed he was one of Mack's brothers. "We was doing a practice run like."

"What?" Mack demanded, grabbing the man by the shoulder and shoving him against the pile of crates.

"Practice, a rehearsal, like. But when we got to the dock, the Gusties were waiting. They done this."

"Fools," Mack pushed him away. Peter understood. Right now, the boat was aflame, but when the fire reached the alcohol, there'd be an explosion. The dock would go up in flames, too.

Meanwhile, the fireman had stepped up. "Mack, we've got to get everyone off the dock. The fire spreads here; it'll all blow." He pointed at the pile of crates.

"Callahan," Mack yelled. "Get off the boat, man. There are gallons of liquor here. It'll all blow in a minute."

The fireman hustled the other men down the dock, away from the fire, past the firetruck, and toward the land. Two of the men carried the unconscious Sean.

Peter was mesmerized by the sight of Bill Callahan struggling to raise the sail while flames licked closer and closer.

"You're a damn fool, Callahan. Get off the boat," Mack yelled.

Peter realized what Bill Callahan was up to. "He's trying to sail the boat away from the dock so the fire doesn't spread," he told Mack. Then, taking a big breath, Peter ran to the dock and jumped to the stern, grabbing a long wooden tiller. "Untie the bow line, Mack," he yelled.

"You're mad!" the big Irishman yelled, but he unwound the line and tossed it to the deck.

Peter steered the tiller to point the bow away. The stern swung toward the dock. Bill finished hoisting the sail, pulled it in, and cleated it. Peter could feel the boat about to move forward when he was pushed down. Mack had jumped on top of him.

"Damned fools." Mack struggled up.

Bill Callahan waved and jumped overboard as the boat slid through the water.

"Where's he going?" Mack's eyes bulged.

Peter grabbed some line and tied up the tiller as the boat slid through the water. "There's the fire boat," he pointed. Mack followed his finger. The big man was still trying to understand when Peter said, "You can swim, can't you?" and shoved his hand straight at Mack's chest, tipping him backward into the cold water.

Chapter Thirty-Eight

I n Kate Gallagher's kitchen, Peter sipped a very hot coffee and pulled at the dry pants belonging to one of Mack's brothers. He and Mack had been fished out by the fireboat and delivered to shore. They'd rushed to the three-decker to get dry and warm. Peter could hear Mack roaring like a lion below as he got the story from his brothers.

One of the firemen came in and sat opposite Peter. Kate handed him a mug and introduced him. "Detective Attwood, this is my husband, Joe." He was the one who'd pointed out the danger of the crates of liquor on the dock. "What happened?" Kate asked, arms akimbo and a frown on her face.

Joe sipped. "Seems the boys've been scheming."

"Scheming? How'd they come to try to burn the dock down?"

"Seems they had the idea they'd smuggle alcohol, come the Volstead Act. So, they bought or borrowed" (Here Kate snickered.) "that boat and they did a test run tonight. Not a dry run, you know. They really met another boat out beyond the harbor and got real whiskey and brought it back." He smelled his coffee and sighed. A cloud formed over his wife's reddening face.

As if to fend off her anger, Joe continued. "Not necessarily a bad idea, mind you, but seems the Gustin Gang over in Southie got wind of it, and they're planning on being a monopoly, as you might say. Although I wonder if the Italians in the North End will agree to that. Still, that's their problem. The Gusties want to be the only Micks in town, so they came over to make Sean McNally an offer. Stop or else." He savored his coffee. "They set the fire as a warning."

"Well, of all the stupid ideas," Kate said. "It's drink will drive them all to the devil. I'm glad they've got the Volstead Act. I say, good enough. Stop these drunk slobs from tearing the place apart. I'm full on done with all of it. Let 'em sober up for the first time in their lazy, stinking lives."

Joe's eyes rose to connect with Peter's, as if to say, "Women!" It was clear to Peter that the fireman thought a local outlet for an occasional drink of liquor was not something to be spurned. But he'd hold his tongue for his lady. Peter had the impression that Kate's husband frequently held his tongue. But perhaps that didn't keep him from doing whatever he wanted.

Mack pounded up the stairs and into the room. "They're a bunch of flaming arseholes, but I'll not have the Wallaces with their Gustin gang coming over here beating them up. Who do those Southie guys think they are?"

"Now, Mack," Kate said, tapping him on the shoulder. "We've had enough excitement tonight. Don't get carried away with you."

He shook her off. "Don't tell me what to do, woman." He looked at Peter. "Are you coming?"

In for a penny, in for a pound, Peter thought to himself. He followed Mack out.

Chapter Thirty-Nine

Downstairs, six men were waiting. Three were Mack's brothers, and the others were friends. They hurried out into a four-door open Model T owned by one of the men. They carried coshes, like the nightsticks carried by policemen, and one had a baseball bat. Tires screeched as they raced through the night.

Peter was squashed in the back seat between a couple of big men while others stood on the running boards, hanging on for dear life at the turns. He had doubts about the excursion. If the Gustin Gang in South Boston had set the fire, they should be arrested. But he doubted Mack had arrest in mind. He wasn't sure what McKenna would think about his participation in what might be a vigilante action. What had he gotten himself into? Perhaps he should have stayed with Mrs. Lee. After all, he had brought her. He hoped she'd found her way home all right, otherwise Dr. Magrath would be angry. *Oh, well. Too late now.*

After bouncing around for half an hour, the car skidded to a stop, and the bodies climbed out. Peter felt he could breathe again as he slid over and out to an empty street. It must be past midnight. The men had surrounded Mack, who was whispering instructions. When he saw Peter, he grabbed him by the arm. "Got your badge?"

Feeling a bit queasy about the implications of the question, Peter pulled the gold badge out of the pocket of the wool knickers he'd borrowed. Were they going to pretend this was a police raid?

Mack grinned. "Come on." He led the way down half a block to a boarded-up building and kicked the door open.

"Raid!" He yelled. "You're surrounded. If you try to exit, my men'll shoot."

Shoot what? Peter thought. Mack's men were armed with baseball bats and nightsticks. Mack probably had led raids like this when he was in the police, and that was why he sounded so authentic. Maybe, in a real police raid, only Mack and his second entered the building, but tonight, there were no armed police outside. Mack probably left the other men waiting outside so the Gustin Gang wouldn't know they weren't armed. This was seeming more and more like a bad idea. Peter gulped. He'd left his pistol at home. It hadn't seemed appropriate for a funeral.

The atmosphere in the dimly lit room tingled with excitement. A bar of rough planks stood before some shelves of bottles. A dingy copper foot rail ran the length of the bar. Large men, skulking under woolen caps, stared at Peter and Mack. Other shadowy figures lurked around the corners of the small room. *Uh oh,* Peter thought. *What are we doing here?*

"Who do ya think you're kidding?" A medium-sized man with a square face and wavy hair parted in the middle stuck his head into the pool of light at the bar. "I heard you were kicked out of the bulls, Mack."

Peter clamped his mouth shut so he wouldn't groan. This guy already knew this wasn't a police raid. *Now, what would happen?*

"Doesn't mean I can't fry you, Frank," Mack growled. "What were you doing in Eastie tonight besides setting fire to the whole damn place?"

Peter could hear feet shuffle as the men in the room moved. *Were they getting ready to attack? He didn't even have a baseball bat. Presumably, this was Frank Wallace, and his men were the Gustin Gang.*

Frank pulled out a silver lighter and played with it on the bar. "That there was a warning, that's all." He looked up straight into Mack's eyes. "This wasn't your idea, was it? Smugglin' booze?" Mack just stared back. "I didn't think so, but them brothers of yours, they're thinkin' of elbowing in on our territory. Just had to make a point before it went too far, if you see what I mean." His furry eyebrows rose in a disingenuous expression of surprise, as if Mack should have expected the attack.

"They're damn fools, but how did you know what they were up to?"

"Ah, I see you didn't. So, how did I know what they were planning when they hadn't told their own big brother? I've got my sources."

Mack pirouetted around the man beside him, snapped open a knife and had Frank with the blade to his throat before anyone else could make a move. Peter felt the hair rise on the back of his neck. He clenched his fists.

The room came to attention. Men sprang forward. But Frank waved an arm at them, and Mack hugged him closer. "What sources?"

"No need to get tetchy," Frank said. "Your old friend, Conor Leary. He's been willing to pass on a hint now and then for enough to keep him in whiskey. Surely, you knew that."

"Leary," Mack said. He frowned. "Leary was working for you? Have you been doing the sabotage to the docks over there, too?"

Frank pulled away, and Mack let him. He was looking at the leader of the Gustin Gang with disbelief. "Conor Leary was working for you?"

Frank straightened his tie, motioning to his men to stay back. He was interested in Mack's reaction. Peter unclenched his fingers.

"Working for us? I wouldn't say that exactly. We helped *him* with a couple of accidents. He paid us well for it."

"Leary?" Mack was really incredulous. "Where would Leary get money to pay you?"

Frank smiled.

Mack's eyes narrowed. "I don't believe you. I say Leary was working for you, and he stopped, so you killed him. Or you sent your goons to beat him up, and they went overboard."

Feet shuffled again in the background. Frank held up a hand. "I don't care what you believe. You need to stay off our territory, and that includes the harbor traffic. Do you need a demonstration?" Tension rose as his men awaited his command.

Mack relaxed. "Ah, yes. You just try it. Don't think I came here alone, do you? Want a real rumble?" He moved his head close to Frank's face and grinned. Peter silently cursed him.

Frank backed away. "Get out of here, you rheumy bastard."

Peter backed toward the door, and Mack spit on the bar, then turned and followed. Peter chugged a big swallow of cold night air when he heard the door bang behind them.

Chapter Forty

The next day, Jake found Peter, Mack, Edwin, and Fanny all gathered around the miniature of the three-decker in the mortuary garage. Peter told him about the previous evening's adventures. Jake knew Mack was a hothead, but he'd hoped the ex-policeman would be a good influence on Peter. Now, he had doubts. He'd rushed off to confront the Gustins and discovered they had set the fire, but what did they learn that helped with the death investigations?

"So, Conor Leary was working for the Gustin Gang," Jake said.

"Leary told them about Mack's brothers' plans to smuggle liquor," Peter said. "Also, the Gustins are responsible for sabotage at the Callahan works."

Mack was staring at the doll house. "Frank Wallace claimed Leary paid them, but they're a bunch of lying turds. I wouldn't believe them." He looked gloomy.

"What's this about your brothers?" Jake asked. He expected the big ex-detective to explode, but Mack just waved a hand as if batting away horse flies. "Dumb assholes."

Peter seemed better informed. He described how he'd seen Mack's brother Sean talking to Sumner at the yacht club.

Jake struggled to understand. "So, Mack's brother bought the big sailboat from Sumner to smuggle liquor once the Volstead Act takes effect. Is that it?"

"I'm not sure they outright bought it," Peter said. "It sounded like they were going into business with Sumner."

It didn't surprise Jake that a businessman like Sumner would find a way to make a profit off Prohibition while maintaining his own secure supply of alcohol. But he didn't see how the dispute between Mack's brothers and the Gustins had to do with the death of Ingrid Ericksson, or even Conor Leary.

Jake wondered if Callahan, Old Will, or Lars could have discovered that Leary was a traitor, sabotaging their business. Would they really have beaten him to death? It would make more sense to fire him and ban him from the works.

"Would Leary really be disloyal to the Callahan family after they'd employed him for so many years?" Fanny asked.

"He was a jealous man," Mack said. "He couldn't stomach that Will and his son had come so far and done so well while he'd made a mess of his life."

Jake thought Mack had a point. He wondered if the ex-detective could see this so clearly because he was busy making a mess of his own life. Who would Mack envy? Peter? His brother Sean? Hadn't Fanny told him the brother stole Mack's sweetheart?

"What if Ingrid saw something and Leary shot her?" Fanny speculated. She pointed at the model house. "You said he was at the scene the day she was shot, didn't you, Mack?"

"He was there when I got there," Mack said.

"Could Leary have come out from the Callahan warehouse, shot her, hidden the rifle in that pile of iron from the railway bridge, and then joined the group around the body?" Fanny asked. "If Lars Ericksson figured it out, he could have beaten Leary for killing his wife."

"Lars was convinced Bill Callahan killed his wife," Peter pointed out. "If he knew it was Leary, why'd he accuse Callahan?"

"Because he's jealous," Fanny told him. "He found a handkerchief with Callahan's initials in Ingrid's drawer and is sure she was involved with Bill. He could have planted the gun in Bill's car."

Jake thought there were too many theories being aired and not enough evidence. "Tell me something," he said. "Why would the Gustin Gang want to sabotage the Callahan company? Why would anyone?"

"Somebody paid them to do it. Ian Stewart, the Sumner manager, said they had some breakage, too," Peter said. "We thought it might be whoever wanted to use the docks to smuggle liquor."

"Mack's brothers?" Jake asked.

"Nah," Mack said. "And yet I didn't know what the stupid dunderheads were up to, but I can't see them sabotaging Callahan."

"Would they pay Leary and the Gustin boys to do it?" Jake asked.

"Never," Mack said. "Where'd they get that kind of money?"

"Maybe the Gustin Gang wanted to use the docks," Peter said. "That would give them a reason."

"Southie's their territory," Mack said. "They're foreigners in Eastie. No, it'd be Conor Leary himself getting revenge on the Callahans."

"What about Sumner?" Fanny asked. "Could he want to drive Callahan out of business?"

"Seems like he planned to run liquor with Mack's brothers," Peter said. "But I can't see him using such dirty tricks."

"Hmph." Mack didn't argue, but he obviously didn't agree. Jake wouldn't put it past the supposedly upright businessman either, but the companies had competed for a long time, so why try to put Callahan out of business now?

Jake decided to put an end to the speculation. "Unless you have something new to add, I think Edwin and I have work to do inside."

"I want to go to the hearing," Fanny said. Jake and the others had no idea what she was talking about. "Oh, you don't know. There's a City Hall meeting about a proposed tunnel over to East Boston. Sumner and Callahan are both bidding on it, but since Bill Callahan is still accused of murder and Old Will has passed away, Eileen Callahan will have to present the bid for Callahan's. I want to see that."

Chapter Forty-One

Peter talked to Edwin before he left. Jake's assistant told him about a new method of identification using fingerprints. Edwin was studying a recent book written by a friend of Jake's who was the police commissioner in Dover, New Hampshire. This system of identification was being used in parts of the prison systems. He told Peter how, in 1911, a New York court had seen a demonstration of fingerprint identification in a burglary case.

"The New York police fingerprint expert took prints from the jury, then one juror put his print on the glass while the expert was out of the room. He convinced the jury when he correctly identified the man's print." Edwin's ruined face glowed with enthusiasm. "I've been experimenting with removing prints from objects."

After further explanation, Peter finally realized that Edwin was saying that he had removed a number of prints from the rifle found in Callahan's automobile, but he had nothing to compare them to.

"Whoever shot Ingrid Ericksson, their prints could be on that gun?" Peter asked.

"There are lots of prints. The police obviously handled the gun when they found it."

"But if Callahan's prints aren't on the gun…"

"Hard to prove a negative," Edwin pointed out. "However, I've identified four sets of prints, I believe. If any of them are *not* from the police, they might be the shooter's. There's a set on the barrel as if the gun was held, not used."

"That could be the person who planted the gun in Callahan's automobile!" Peter said. He thought hard. McKenna hated Dr. Magrath, but he seemed to fear the powerful medical examiner. Peter had managed to get the gun away from the police. Could he get the fingerprints Edwin needed for comparison? Peter was sure that McKenna had planted the gun. Whether it was just to spite Magrath, or to help someone else, Peter's superior had framed Callahan. If McKenna refused to cooperate, that might tell them something.

After consulting Jake, Peter, and Edwin headed to the police station. Jake doubted a court would accept fingerprint evidence, but he liked the idea of bothering McKenna. Peter wasn't sure it was good for his career to side with Magrath over the chief detective of his division, but it was too late. He'd already chosen sides.

McKenna growled when Peter introduced Edwin and stated that Dr. Magrath had sent them to take fingerprints from any police officers who had touched the rifle.

"What do you think you're up to?" The florid-faced chief detective narrowed his eyes. "If that dirty corpse slicer thinks he's going to make trouble, he's got another thing coming. Is he doubting what we found? Oh, I see. You want to accuse me and my man Jerry of planting that gun, don't you? Well, you'd be wrong about that." He got up and stomped to his open door. "Jerry, get in here!"

"Boss?" A broad-shouldered bull of a man in shirtsleeves came to the door. Peter was taken aback that McKenna was so quick to comply.

"Get in here. This rookie and Magrath's monkey here think we planted that gun in Callahan's motor. You and me were the only ones touched that piece the other night, right? They want to see our fingers."

Peter watched as Edwin pulled out an inkpad and rolled each finger of each man from inkpad to white paper. He couldn't believe McKenna was being so cooperative. He even seemed a bit interested in the procedure.

When Edwin finished, McKenna dismissed Jerry and swore as he wiped his fingers on a handkerchief. Then, with a crafty look in his eye, he grabbed a pile of notes and shuffled through them till he got one that he threw across the table at Edwin. "Take that back to your boss. It's the message we got that night that sent us over to that yacht club. Hah!"

Peter grabbed the sheet. It was a note from the on-duty sergeant. "Call received. Man says gun that shot woman in Eastie in Callahan's Ford at Eastern Yacht Club in Marblehead. Refused to give name."

Could it be possible that McKenna *hadn't* planted the gun?

Chapter Forty-Two

Fanny's friend Cornelia guided her through the maze of city hall to a hearing room on the second floor. Tall windows lit the room. Men in suits milled around, divided into two primary groups. Cornelia spotted her son-in-law, Peter's father, and Peter himself on the left side of the room. She and Fanny joined them. Peter looked downcast. Turning away from his father, Peter described how he and Edwin had visited the police station. He worried that Chief Detective McKenna was even more determined to get him fired.

Augustus Sumner was the center of attention on the left side of the room. He was surrounded by Beacon Hill men in wool suits, looking satisfied and superior. Opposite them, Fanny recognized Eileen Callahan in her tall hat. She stood between former mayor Honey Fitz and a troop of his followers. In the middle of the room, a third group of men frowned and shrugged their shoulders. They looked angry.

Peter ushered his grandmother and Fanny to seats. He seemed gloomy. "Bill Callahan is still being prosecuted. He's out on bail, but it was considered bad form for him to show up, so his wife will present their proposal. Callahan's company wants to bid for the contract for a tunnel, and so does Sumner."

"I thought your father and Gus Sumner were rivals," Fanny commented.

"In sailboats. Ashore, they tend to cling together with the others," Peter nodded. "They're determined that the old established Sumner name needs to be on the tunnel, not those upstart Callahans."

It was a face-off. The Beacon Hill Brahmin culture against the Irish

Catholics of Boston. In Chicago, where Fanny had grown up, there were Irish American politicians but plenty of Italian, German, and Polish factions as well. Wealthy industrialists formed a top echelon of society in the city— people like her parents. But they were nowhere near as haughty and arrogant as the Brahmins of Boston, who didn't seem to realize how insolent they seemed to everyone else.

"Who're the people in the middle?" Fanny asked.

"Businessmen who are furious that the ferry service is so bad between the city and East Boston," Peter said. They watched as Peter's father drifted over to the middle group and pulled a short man in a striped suit to the side. "A lot of them are clients of the bank, too," he added.

A group of men filed in to sit behind a long table in the front of the room. "This joint commission is split between city and state representatives," Cornelia told Fanny. "Mayor Peters is in favor of the Sumner faction, but some of the city representatives still back the Callahan faction. The state reps on the left are mostly for Sumner."

Everyone turned toward the commission. "Mrs. Callahan has quite a group to convince," Fanny said. She didn't envy Eileen Callahan's task. Would the completely male commission deign to listen to a woman? Fanny hoped so.

Mayor Peters pounded the gavel and introduced the board members, then summed up the meeting agenda. "This hearing is to address the request for better service on the ferries." The businessmen in the middle of the room applauded with comments like "about time" and "come on now." They didn't stand on their dignity. Unlike the Brahmins, who seemed to look down their noses at the crowd. Fanny thought the noisy businessmen behaved a lot more like a crowd in Chicago would have done.

The mayor continued. "Since investigation has shown that a tunnel can be made a reality more speedily than any ferry service to East Boston can be bolstered up, we have asked for preliminary bids to be submitted."

The crowd in the middle groaned and muttered angrily. One man stood up and said, "This tunnel idea is just administration 'hush-darling' propaganda, put out to minimize criticism of a bad ferry problem." A small cheer greeted his speech. They didn't believe the investigation. They thought it was just a ploy on the part of the politicians. Fanny wondered if that was true.

Mayor Peters pounded his gavel. "You know that's not true. We can have a tunnel to East Boston in a relatively short time; that's the truth. Even if we put forty-five boats on the route, perfect service couldn't be achieved. Up and downstream traffic, fogs, and mechanical disruptions interfere with ferry service."

Fanny remembered her ferry ride over to East Boston. No wonder the impatient businessmen were frustrated. It was such a short ride across the inner harbor. But she could picture the waterway clogged with boats cutting across the routes used by huge tankers and cruise liners. What a mess. No wonder the administrators who had to take a longer view wanted a tunnel.

"The Waterways Commission and Transit Department, after painstaking investigation, recommend a tunnel, and we will hear proposals today." Mayor Peters pounded again. "A representative from the Callahan company is invited to present their proposal."

There was a hush. Everyone knew that the founder of the Callahan company had passed away and the current president was under indictment for murder.

Ushered by one of Honey Fitz's followers, Eileen stepped up to the podium facing the table full of men. She arranged her papers in front of her. She took a breath, and Fanny could see her clutch the edge of the podium.

"Gentlemen, thank you for this opportunity to present our proposal. If you will permit, we have a diagram to show you." She pointed to an easel that held two large diagrams on huge cardboard placards, one on each side, so the audience could see the same thing the board was viewing. It showed a sketchy map of the harbor with a line between two sides and a loop at each end.

"We propose a four-way tunnel between East Boston and the city proper. It is a double-barrel tunnel of two roadways enabling four lines of vehicles to proceed, two in each direction. The engineers' report points out that a single roadway would be held to the speed of horse-drawn vehicles. With four ways, motor traffic can pass horse-drawn vehicles."

It was ingenious. Fanny had seen how the mix of horse and motor-drawn cars caused havoc in the narrow old streets of Boston. Giving the faster motorcars their own lane would certainly be more efficient. The crowd muttered. The noise became loud enough that the mayor struck the gavel again for order.

Eileen seemed to be getting into her stride. "One of the biggest objections to a tunnel is the fear that a grade on either end would bring entrances as far away from both waterfronts as Scollay Square in town and Central Square in East Boston. These loops at the ends will allow entrances and exits near the waterfront instead."

Cornelia tapped Fanny's arm and explained in her ear. "The tunnel must be dug deep below the harbor. The ends have to rise gradually. By making it a loop, instead of a straight line, the tunnel entrance and exit can be nearer the harbor, not a mile away." Fanny nodded. It was another ingenious solution.

Then, Eileen announced the projected cost of over ten million dollars to be paid over thirty years. The murmurs became expressions of horror. Fanny thought Eileen had done a good job presenting the Callahan proposal, but the honest declaration of the money needed to fund it scandalized the crowd.

Over the uproar, the mayor thanked the Callahan company and invited Sumner to present his proposal. Sumner looked tall and imposing as he replaced Mrs. Callahan. Fanny couldn't help rooting for Eileen. She hoped her arguments wouldn't be overlooked just because she was a female pitted against a very self-assured male.

Sumner gestured to the diagrams and admitted they addressed some of the issues with a tunnel. He also agreed that the cost of the construction would be substantial and would need to be funded by the state and city over several decades. His main argument, however, was not about the specifics of the project but on the ability of his company to sustain the work over a number of years.

"As you are all aware, the Sumner Company has been in East Boston since it was Noddle Island. My ancestors developed the land, and my family continues to invest in this part of the city. The city and state can be assured that the Sumner Company will continue to exist and thrive."

Fanny saw Peter roll his eyes. She knew from Cornelia that Peter had grown up with this assumption that the past was the stone foundation of civil society. The Brahmins believed the incoming hordes of immigrants were bent on tearing that structure down, and they were determined to defend it. In Chicago, everyone was an interloper, including the adventurers from the East Coast who came to the Midwest to strike riches. They certainly resisted the incoming immigrants from Europe, but the core society group was less firmly packed than here in Boston. Here, they seemed overly impressed by ancestors who had stepped off the *Mayflower* into the primitive wilderness of Plymouth. Chicago was more impressed by the mountain of wealth a man had built up himself.

Sumner went on the attack. "I am sorry to have to point out that the Callahan Company is in peril at this moment. Would you trust your tens of millions of dollars to a firm where the founder is gone and the incumbent is accused of murder? And, as if that weren't enough, I need to tell you that the Callahan company has been subjected to a series of misfortunes. Far be it from me, gentlemen, to accuse a rival firm of incompetence, but a series of collapsing wharves, equipment failures, and dock fires must call into question the wisdom of choosing to place the public trust in the Callahan organization. I'm sorry, but it's true. These things happened."

The murmurs came near to a roar as Mayor Peters hammered his gavel again. Fanny saw some men rise and circle Eileen, talking vigorously to Honey Fitz, while on Sumner's side, there were smiles of satisfaction. Sumner himself gave a little bow and retreated to a seat among his followers. One of them was Peter's father, who nodded at Sumner. Fanny was disgusted by how smug they appeared.

As Mayor Peters sent some staff to wrangle people back to their seats, Honey Fitz stepped to the podium. Fanny knew he was an old rival of the current mayor, but apparently, he was still a man who couldn't be ignored. Two of the board members demanded he be heard. Reluctantly, Peters allowed it.

"Thank you, sirs." Honey Fitz was short compared to Sumner and even Eileen, but the former mayor had a warm smile and a twinkle in his eye. "Now, I'd not want to be contradicting our old friend Sumner from his old, distinguished family, but this is a very new construction this tunnel we're considering. As you may not know, the Callahan Company played a part in the building of the current tunnel for the trains. In 1904 Old Will Callahan had the building of the conduits that take the electricity through so the trains'll run at all."

Fanny wanted to cheer him on.

He smiled around the room at all of them. "I'd never want to disparage a name that came over with those intrepid fellows on those early boats like the *Mayflower*. Why that's the same as me own dad, who also sailed the perilous seas to get here. But, since we're reviewing past problems, I just have to jiggle your memories a bit to have you recall a terrible accident at the Sumner docks a couple of years ago now, when the collapse killed three of the workmen."

Fanny hadn't heard of this accident, but it seemed that everyone else in the room remembered it. Horror from Sumner's side of the room, snide remarks from the Callahan side, and grumbles from the middle caused the mayor to pound the gavel again. Honey Fitz waved a hand. "That's all I'm going to say now, all I have. Just remember." He smiled sweetly.

Peter whispered in Fanny's ear. "My father isn't very happy with all this. Look." He nodded at the elder Attwood, who had moved a few seats away from Sumner's group, and caught the eye of the man in the striped suit he'd been talking to before the meeting. Was he abandoning Sumner to throw his support to the group that wanted more ferries?

A red-faced Sumner strode to the podium and demanded to be heard. Mayor Peters recognized him.

"I absolutely deny any responsibility for the tragedy that was so treacherously described. The Sumner Company was never accused of negligence..."

"They bought off the families," Peter whispered to Fanny.

"...Furthermore, I want to announce that the manager for this tunnel project will be Mr. Lars Ericksson, who formerly was employed by the Callahan Company but has joined Sumner when he lost confidence in the diligence and responsibility of his employer after the death of its founder. I tell you, gentlemen, if even old employees are leaving an organization, how can you dare to entrust public funds to it? You can't. Sumner Company is the only rightful winner of this project."

"Uh oh," Peter said as he and Fanny watched Ian Stewart, current manager of the Sumner Company, march out of the room. Peter also pointed at his own father, who was nodding vigorously at the man in the striped suit.

That man approached the podium as Sumner turned away. Mayor Peters recognized him when he said he had an alternate proposal.

The uproar quieted as he proposed the city scrape up one million dollars to buy new ferryboats, now costing two hundred seventy-five thousand dollars apiece, and to rebuild slips and docks. The mayor protested that such a move was out of the question as the city was "up to its neck" in debt as it was. But when more speakers and organizations got up and expressed themselves in favor of getting something done quickly to relieve a bad situation, the mayor dissolved the meeting with a promise to start something.

"Looks like the tunnel project is scrapped," Cornelia said. "That's a surprise."

Fanny thought so, too. Neither Eileen nor Sumner had won the day. The ferry proponents took over the meeting and destroyed their hopes. "The former mayor certainly stirred things up," Fanny said to Cornelia.

"Ah, Honey Fitz, he's quite the one for quick thinking. They say Henry Cabot Lodge once told him he was impudent and asked him if he thought Jews and Italians had any right to be in this country. Fitz told him, 'As much as your father or mine. It was only a difference of a few ships.' That's what all the *Mayflower* talk was about."

Fanny laughed.

"Oh, yes," Cornelia continued. "There's a little ditty about him. 'Honey Fitz can talk you blind / on any subject you can find / Fish and fishing, motor boats / Railroads, streetcars, getting votes.'"

Chapter Forty-Three

Outside the meeting room, Peter caught up with Ian Stewart. The short Scottish man looked downcast. Peter took him by the arm and walked him down the stairs and out the door to a bench where Ian could dig out his pipe and bag of tobacco. Peter could see he needed it.

"I can't believe he'd do that to me," Ian said.

Peter could believe it. Treachery, in support of profit, was a way of life for his father and his father's friends, like Sumner. "If it's any comfort, I doubt Sumner will get the contract. I saw my father give the go-ahead to the man who proposed more ferries."

Ian looked puzzled.

"It's my father playing both sides of the street," Peter said. "He was bankrolling Sumner's bid but, when that hit the skids, he had a backup plan. I'm sure his bank will fund new ferries instead. He's no more loyal to Sumner than Sumner was to you."

Ian just looked depressed. "But Lars Ericksson. He's a carpenter for heaven's sake, not a project manager." A cap of gloom seemed to settle on the little man's head.

Peter felt sorry for him. "To bring up that catastrophe. That was unfair." Peter thought the deaths of three men must weigh on Ian. What a horrible memory. He knew it must be terribly painful, but he couldn't help asking. "What happened?"

Ian shivered. "It was three years ago." He paused, bringing up the memories. "It was Sumner who insisted we buy pine planks for the job. I'd told him it wasn't right, but he didn't listen. They'd built the scaffolding for the L dock, and then, when three of them fools climbed up all together, it collapsed. Into the freezing water. We tried to get them out." He shook his head as if trying to rid himself of the picture.

"It's not like God almighty Sumner was there himself, you know. Not him. Off at some lunch or concert or something. He wasn't even around. So, I got the blame, as usual. Me. I had to tell the widows. They cursed me."

Peter patted the man on the back. Ian shrugged him off. Peter was about to leave him to his misery when the Sumner manager spoke again. "I saw that double-crossing Swede the day she was shot."

Peter stopped. "You saw Lars Ericksson? Where?"

Ian puffed on his pipe. "In the yard," he muttered. He took the pipe from his mouth and looked up at Peter. His eyes were dark with a cold anger. "In the yard. My office has a window looking out on the yard."

"Did he have a gun?" Peter was picturing Lars at the corner of the Callahan building, shooting up at his wife.

Ian looked away. "No. He was by the storage box."

Perhaps he had shot and then hid the gun in the storage box. "Did you hear a shot?"

"No. I was just coming back to my office from doing inventory in the storage room," he said.

Peter was excited. "Are you saying you think Lars shot his wife? Why didn't you say before?"

"Aw, I was sorry for the man. He was sure she was cheatin' on him, and I took pity. He found a handkerchief that was Callahan's, and he was wild with jealousy. He's a dark Nordic soul that one. But I sympathized. He thought she betrayed him. Betrayal's a wound cuts deep and infects the soul."

Ian was thinking of his own experience of betrayal by Sumner. He mumbled on. "That's why Lars put the rifle in Callahan's Ford. He hates him and wants to ruin him for what he did with Ingrid. It serves the adulterer right; they're all of them evil. Sumner, Ericksson, they're as bad as Callahan; they're all evil men."

Ian hadn't told them what he saw the day Ingrid died because he, too, believed that she had betrayed her husband with Callahan. But Peter knew

Callahan wasn't Ingrid's lover. Mack was. He hesitated to share that information with the Scottish man, but he hated to hear the man's injured ramblings. Peter saw a shine in Ian's eyes. Tears? He felt a need to reach out a hand and pull the man back from the brink. "It wasn't Callahan," he blurted.

Ian turned shiny eyes up at him. Silent.

"It was Mack. Mack was seeing Ingrid, not Callahan. He admitted it, but since we didn't think it would help Callahan with the police, at least not now, we didn't advertise it."

Ian stared. "Lars was so sure. He had the handkerchief he got from her. He told me how he pulled it away from her and screamed at her. He was convinced it was Bill Callahan. She refused to answer him."

"So he planted that rifle in Callahan's car," Peter said.

"Yes. I believe so," Ian said. "Was it really that big Irishman she was with?"

Peter was sure it was a mistake to tell the man about Mack. "Don't tell anyone, okay? There's no reason to ruin her reputation, and Lars is a dangerous man."

What did it mean that Ian had seen Lars in the yard the day of Ingrid's death? Lars had claimed he was in the kitchen when she fell from the porch. No one had questioned his testimony. But now Peter had a witness to say he was in the yard. Ian hadn't seen or heard a gun, but still…

Ian grabbed Peter's arm. "I saw Sumner and Leary. I saw Sumner give him money. Then he was dead, and now Lars is getting a job from Sumner."

Peter was surprised. Ian had never mentioned Leary before. The man had been beaten to death and left in the dumpster after Ingrid's death. The old drunk had been present when they found Ingrid's body. How did Ian know Conor Leary anyhow? Leary worked for Callahan, not the Sumner Company. "When did you see Leary with your boss?"

"Some weeks ago," Ian said. "It was right before the accidents started happening at Callahan's."

Peter thought about it. Had Sumner paid Leary to stage the accidents and hire the Gustin gang to help? It made sense. Maybe all along, Sumner had been planning for the tunnel project. He wanted to be able to stand up at the meeting and destroy Callahan's chances of getting the contract. "Are you saying Sumner paid him to do the sabotage? He's using those accidents to try and get this tunnel project by making Callahan look bad."

Ian frowned. "I'd never have thought it of Sumner. He's always so sure that the fact that he's got the old name and the old firm that there's nothing Callahan could do to compete. I never thought he needed to sabotage Callahan. But I never thought he'd hire Lars over me either."

"It's a new world, and the plans for that tunnel were obviously well thought out. Sumner might have found out Callahan would have an edge in the engineering part of it," Peter said.

"Aye. Sumner has little respect for engineers. Now, Callahan, he's got some kind of certificate for civil engineering. I told Sumner I should go for that, but he wouldn't pay for it." Ian stuck his pipe in his mouth and puffed angrily.

Peter continued to speculate. Maybe Sumner was paying Leary. But Leary wanted more money. Maybe he threatened to expose Sumner. Sumner had to shut him up. But it was hard to imagine Sumner dirtying his nice suit to beat a man to death. He'd seen Sumner cheat or use dirty tricks in a boat race, but he'd never heard of him having a physical fight. He would have to get someone else to do it. "How does Sumner know Lars Ericksson?" he asked.

"I knew Sumner talked to Lars about coming over to the company," Ian said. "He's the best ship's carpenter around. He's no engineer, though. And no manager. He barely speaks English, for God's sake."

Peter looked down at Ian, thinking that Sumner could have persuaded Lars to get rid of Leary for him. Maybe bringing him in to run the big tunnel project was his reward. Peter thought he needed to talk to someone about his theory. Not McKenna, he'd never listen. But Dr. Magrath might. "Maybe Sumner owed Lars Ericksson for something."

Ian took his pipe from his mouth and looked up at Peter. "What a sly, dirty dog."

Chapter Forty-Four

After the hearing broke up, Fanny and Cornelia found Peter outside the building. He seemed worried. "It's Sumner," he told them. "I'm sure he did it. Ian Stewart saw him give Conor Leary money." He pointed at the retreating back of the little Scottish man.

So that was what Peter was doing when he left the hearing. He had followed Ian out of the room and talked to him. As they listened to Peter recount his conversation with the Sumner manager, Fanny saw the young detective had a lot of sympathy for Ian because he'd been blamed for the tragic deaths three years ago, and then, suddenly, he was also replaced on a potential big project by Lars. She wondered if Peter realized the man's bitterness could have colored his story.

"So, you can see why it must be Sumner, right?"

Cornelia glanced at Fanny as if she thought her grandson was losing his mind. "What did he do?"

Peter bit his lip. "I think he's the one who had Leary killed. He must have gotten Lars Ericksson to do it. McKenna will never believe it."

Fanny wondered how Peter had suddenly jumped to the conclusion that the Brahmin businessman got the big Swede to kill a man. She doubted it. She just didn't believe Lars was violent. He was deeply sad and in despair. She saw that in him. But she had never believed he killed his wife.

Peter was determined to find a villain in Sumner. Fanny found the arrogant Brahmin objectionable, but that didn't mean he was a killer. Peter was biased, although he might not realize it. He liked the young Callahan couple, and he disliked Sumner, who reminded him of his father. He felt sympathy for poor Ian Stewart and antipathy for Lars Ericksson. He was determined to prove his superior McKenna wrong about Callahan while protecting Mack's secret relationship with Ingrid. Watching him pace back and forth in front of the bench, she thought he needed some help to see clearly. "Why don't we go and talk to Dr. Magrath?" she suggested.

Cornelia worried about her grandson. "Peter, Mr. Sumner is a prominent man in the city. Chief McKenna won't let you accuse him unless you have very strong evidence. And even then..."

Peter was sorrowful. "That's just the problem. Someone like Sumner is surrounded by protections, his wealth, his old family, his business connections. It makes him untouchable, while someone like Callahan can be destroyed in one swoop. It's wrong."

It was wrong, but Peter was frighteningly naïve in his assumption that wrongs could be easily righted by blurting out an accusation. "Come along and see Dr. Magrath, Peter. He'll know how to deal with this." To her and Cornelia's relief, the young man readily agreed.

Edwin let them in, and they found Jake in his office. Fanny described the tunnel hearing. "Eileen Callahan did a good job, standing in for her husband, but Sumner got up and claimed the Callahan company couldn't be relied on, then Honey Fitz turned the argument against Sumner based on an accident on the wharves that got some of his workers killed. The local businessmen are up in arms and want more ferries instead of a tunnel..." She told him about Sumner hiring Lars Ericksson to be project manager for the tunnel.

Jake cocked an eyebrow. "Sounds like a typical political fiasco. Mudslinging. With Callahan accused of murder, they'd never award the contract to him anyway, but it sounds like Honey Fitz managed to throw a spanner in the works for Sumner. He won't get the contract either."

"What if Sumner's behind the sabotage at Callahan's works?" Peter asked. Fanny knew he was bursting to share his theories with the medical examiner. "Ian Stewart told me he saw Sumner with Leary, the dead man. He saw money exchanged. Leary could have been behind the sabotage. Sumner could have hired him to do it so he could get the tunnel contract."

Jake was skeptical. "If Sumner hired Leary to do sabotage, perhaps Leary turned around and tried to extort more money from him. But do you really think Augustus Sumner took an iron bar, beat the man to death, and then heaved him into the storage bin? I can't see Sumner getting blood on his three-piece suit," Jake said.

Peter's face was red with excitement. "But Lars would. Listen, Stewart also said he saw Lars in the yard the day his wife was shot!"

"With a gun?" Jake asked.

"No, but it was after she fell. He could have hidden the rifle."

Jake sat back, assessing the excited young detective. "I should point out that we know Lars Ericksson's rifle did not kill Ingrid. And why didn't Ian Stewart tell anyone about seeing Lars before this?"

Fanny could see that Peter was losing his audience. She also doubted Peter's theory. "Did Sumner have a rifle?" she asked.

Peter whirled around, and his eyes lit up. "That's it. Maybe he let Lars use a gun. Then he would know Lars had shot his wife, so when he needed to get rid of Leary, he could hold that over Lars and make him do it." Jake and Fanny were unconvinced. It frustrated him. "That's why he'd give Lars that job on the big tunnel project. He owed him."

"That's a large amount of speculation with very little evidence," Jake pointed out.

Fanny could see that Jake was disappointed in the young detective. She hoped he would not reject his new pupil. "What did Edwin find out about the fingerprints on the rifle that was used to shoot Ingrid?" she asked.

They called in Edwin, who told them he had matched prints from McKenna and one of his men, but there were still unidentified prints on the barrel of the rifle.

"Lars Ericksson," Peter said. He looked triumphant.

"No," Edwin said. "We have his prints from his own rifle, and they do not match."

"Wait, I know. They must be Sumner's. He could have put the rifle in Callahan's motorcar at the yacht club that night."

"We don't have Mr. Sumner's fingerprints," Edwin told him.

"We don't even know if Sumner had a rifle," Jake pointed out.

"I can find out," Peter said. "I'm sure Stewart will know, and I'm sure I can get something with Sumner's fingerprints."

"If you do, I can compare them," Edwin told him. Jake's assistant was always the impartial scientist. Unlike Peter, he didn't care which man was guilty. He just wanted to use his newfound skills to identify and convict the right man. Or woman, Fanny supposed. It was interesting how differently each of them approached the problem. But both were fervent. She hoped Jake realized that, even if they made mistakes, they were learning to investigate in a way that was different from how McKenna and his ilk would do it.

Peter echoed her thoughts. "McKenna will never consider Sumner a suspect. He'd arrest Ericksson if he had to admit he was wrong about Callahan, but he'd never even interrogate a Brahmin like Sumner."

"Nonsense, even McKenna can't ignore evidence. But you have no evidence, just speculation," Jake told him.

"Sumner's rifle. Sumner's fingerprints. We can get evidence," Peter insisted.

Edwin stood back to let the young policeman pass. "A glass he held in his hand would be a good source for fingerprints," he told Peter, who nodded as he rushed away.

Jake watched him leave. "Hope springs eternal," he told Fanny.

Chapter Forty-Five

Peter took a trolley to East Boston and walked to the Sumner warehouse on Border Street, across from the docks. He stood for a moment, looking up the steep hill to the rear of the Callahan mansion that was on Meridian Street. Backstairs zigzagged down a steep hill. Halfway down on the left was the three-decker where Mack and his brothers lived and where Ingrid had fallen to her death.

Below, he stood between the Callahan and Sumner companies. To his left, he saw the blackened brick of the Callahan works with the storage bin and the creepy iron skeleton of an old railroad bridge lying in a heap beside it. Across from the rusted spider web of iron, the concrete side of the Sumner Company building sat. There was a large window with six big panes near the street but overlooking the Callahan works. That would be Ian Stewart's office with a view of the side of the Callahan property.

Even here, there was a stratified order. The comparatively wealthy Callahans occupied the top of the hill, with the rickety tenement below and the workaday warehouses across from the docks that were the lifeblood of the community. Peter could imagine the McNallys and Gallaghers and Erickssons trying to crawl up that hill to prosperity while Callahan, having reached that peak, aspired to climb the impossible heights of Beacon Hill where a man like Sumner was at home. Having begun his own life elbow to elbow with people like Sumner, Peter had only recently realized the immense anthill that supported life at the top.

He liked Bill and Eileen Callahan, and he had liked Old Will, especially after hearing stories of the man's life at the wake. The society he saw there was teeming compared to the austere atmosphere of his own family and classmates, but it seemed so much more alive. Dirty, noisy, but alive. Even if his failure to resolve these murders got him fired from the police force, he knew he couldn't go back to the cold marble atmosphere of his father's bank. It wasn't for him.

A side door in the Sumner building opened, and Ian Stewart beckoned him in. Looking both ways as if guilty, he ushered Peter into an office with a high ceiling stacked with boxes and filing cabinets. A moderately sized desk was placed at right angles to the window. Peter could see the iron pieces and the storage bin beside the Callahan warehouse. If he moved to the lefthand corner, he could just see the edge of the building and a portion of the three-decker where Ingrid had been shot.

He explained his dilemma to Ian.

"You need to prove the rifle was Sumner's?" He scratched his head. "Aye, he has a gun cabinet. Most everyone does down here. Sometimes the rats come up from the water, and it's the best way to get rid of the boldest of them." He dropped into his chair. "But even if it *is* his gun, you'll never get the authorities to accuse him. He has too much influence," Ian said.

Peter could tell he despaired of anyone listening, so he tried to explain Edwin's work with fingerprints. Ian looked puzzled.

"If we could find something, say a glass he had held in his hand, Edwin could match it to fingers that held the barrel of the rifle that we know was planted in Callahan's motorcar. But first, can we look at this gun cabinet, see if there's a rifle there?"

Ian shrugged and stood, taking a bunch of keys from his pocket. He led the way to a corridor that led to a larger office on the other side with a big mahogany desk and an oriental rug on the floor. A cabinet sat against one wall. Ian unlocked it. They found two pistols, a shotgun, and ammunition for a rifle, but no rifle.

Peter was excited. "You're sure there was a rifle?"

Ian was less excited. "Yes. I've seen one. But it's not often we open this, and he could say he took it home to his place on the north shore."

Peter was sure he was on to something. "Is there anything with his fingerprints? A glass?"

Ian locked up the cabinet and stepped to a side table with a bottle and cut-glass tumblers. "He'd use these for a nip, but they're kept washed and ready."

Peter sighed and looked around. "Anything else..."

Ian was staring at the side table. "He's due in any minute." He paused. "He wants to see Lars. He even left me a message to get Lars over here. Let's do this." He picked up the bottle and glasses and set them on the desk. "Perhaps that'll give him the idea for a drink to celebrate."

Peter thought the words were bitter. Ian was furious that Lars was being hired. He must have feared for his own position. Peter had a lot of sympathy for the man. But if Sumner was a killer, surely Ian's job would be affected anyhow. At least the little Scot could have some revenge on his treacherous employer.

"Come along, let's get you out of here before Mr. Sumner arrives." Ian led the way to a side door near his office. "I'll get Mr. Ericksson to come and see Mr. Sumner. You can stay away. No doubt Kate Gallagher can give you a cup of tea."

They crossed the yard, avoiding the rusting iron pieces that littered the Callahan property. At the three-decker, Peter knocked on Kate Gallagher's second-floor rooms and found Mack seated at her kitchen table looking downcast. Peter had told Ian he would wait as long as it took to get the glass with Sumner's fingerprints. If their plan worked.

Chapter Forty-Six

Kate rushed around, getting a fresh pot of tea and a slightly chipped teacup for Peter. He had the impression he'd interrupted a dispute. Mack was slightly red in the face and stared into his tea mug. Kate huffed and puffed.

Peter cleared his throat. "Thanks. I'm waiting for something." He wanted to tell Mack what he'd learned, but he hesitated to share the information with Kate. He'd profited from her gossip himself, but he didn't want his suspicions about Sumner to be public yet.

Kate couldn't contain herself. She appeared to have accepted Peter as a friend of the family, or perhaps another brother. She wanted to have him learn from Mack's mistakes. "It's a sorry day when a man can't keep himself from his neighbor's wife." She crossed her arms on her chest and glared at her brother. Mack stared into his tea. Peter wondered if he was reading the leaves to see his future.

Kate continued. "I know she was a flirt. We all knew that. But to take her up on it. What kind of a man does that? And then to let Lars believe it was Bill. Did you *tell* him it was Bill?"

When Mack just hunched down more, Peter came to his defense. "Mack didn't need to tell him anything. Lars found one of Bill's handkerchiefs and confronted her with it. We think Lars was the one who shot her. But Mack didn't do anything."

"What? What handkerchief? What did you do?" She turned her fury on Mack.

Mack rose up like a mountain. "I knew it," he growled. "That cold bastard, he did it. He shot Ingrid."

When Kate began scolding him again, he stomped out of the kitchen. They could hear his heavy footsteps on the stairs.

"For the love of God, he's going to go kill Lars," Kate shouted.

"It's all right," Peter rose and put a hand on her shoulder. "Ian Stewart took Lars over to see Sumner. I heard them leave. He's not there."

Sure enough, they heard Mack pound down the stairs again.

Kate exhaled and dropped into the chair Mack had left. "Fools. All of them. What a bunch of fools." She looked at Peter and asked sharply, "What's this about a handkerchief?"

Peter told her how Lars had found one embroidered with Bill Callahan's initials. It enraged him.

Kate rolled her eyes. She got up heavily and stepped to the doorway. Beside the door, a wicker basket was piled with white cloth. She snatched a piece. "Like this?" she asked, waving a white handkerchief in Peter's face. "Ingrid had Bill's handkerchief, is that it? Not likely. I have Bill's handkerchiefs, and Eileen's and Old Will's. I do cleaning and repairing of their fine linen. If there was any handkerchief of Bill's around, it was stolen from my work basket. There's been one missing for weeks. I argued with Eileen about it, the poor soul. She insisted I lost one, and I told her it was her own fault. Why would Bill give Ingrid a handkerchief? To wipe her nose? She had no handkerchief unless she stole it and if she were doing that, she'd have taken one of Eileen's with the lace and all. These men! Fools! All of them!"

Peter looked at the basket by the door. Every time he'd been in the house, that door had remained open. Kate kept track of everything that went on in the building. He knew that. Anyone could have taken a handkerchief, just as she said. But why would they?

Chapter Forty-Seven

Peter sipped his tea as Kate continued to complain about Mack and his brothers. It was a relief when Ian Stewart appeared at the door with a cloth bag in his hand. "Here it is. I've got to get back, but that glass was in Sumner's hand. He's still talking to Lars, celebrating his coming on to the payroll."

Peter knew it galled the Sumner manager that his Brahmin employer had hired the big Swede. He wasn't surprised when Ian rushed away. Peter felt the tumbler through the cloth bag. He hoped Edwin would be able to match the fingerprints to the ones on the rifle that had shot Ingrid Ericksson.

Kate sniffed. "That one," she said, nodding at the doorway where Ian Stewart had been. "He looks down his nose at us, as if he's any better. He hates Bill Callahan for succeeding where his employer, Sumner, fails. Bill's a hustler, that's true, but that's what it takes, isn't it?" She got up and bent over the table to look through the window. Ian was hurrying back to the Sumner warehouse.

"Sumner nearly fired Stewart after that accident with three men killed. Did you know that?" she asked. She sat back down. "Don't know why he was kept on. He's a sneak that Ian Stewart. What's this I heard about Lars and the Sumner company?"

Peter told her how Sumner was hiring Lars away from Callahan.

"You mean to tell me after all this baloney about that handkerchief, Lars is going to leave the company that fed him and his family for all these years because he's got it in his head that Ingrid was seeing Bill? Well, it's about time Mack set him straight on that." She frowned. She was angry with her brother.

Peter was surprised at her vehement dislike for Ian Stewart. He thought the Scottish and Irish would be allies against the British. Apparently, not once they got to the New World anyhow. Of course, there was a difference in religions. Strait-laced Presbyterians took a dim view of Roman Catholicism. Should he explain to Kate that he believed Sumner was the killer? They heard pounding on the stairs.

Ian Stewart stuck his head in the doorway. "You've got to come. He's killed Lars. Lars is dead on the floor, and Sumner is gone."

"Good Lord," Kate said. She gripped the table as if she were dizzy.

Peter followed Ian down the stairs and across the yard. He could hear Kate calling after them. They rushed to the side door to the Sumner warehouse, then past Ian's office and into the larger owner's office at the back.

Bill Callahan was covered with blood, sitting on the floor, Lars Ericksson's head in his lap.

Mack hovered in the background. "It's Lars. He's gone. Someone's killed him, same as Leary." He pointed at a chunk of iron on the floor. It dripped blood on the carpet. "I've called Magrath and the station."

Chapter Forty-Eight

J ake stared at the scene in the Sumner company's office. It was a bloody mess. Chief McKenna was stomping back and forth between the huge desk and the elaborate tripod setup that Edwin had erected over the body of the dead man. Bill Callahan slumped on one of the chairs against a wall, with a policeman hovering over him. Callahan's shirt and jacket were stained with rusty blood. It would be enough for McKenna to jump to the conclusion that Callahan had killed Lars Ericksson.

Mack hulked in a corner, his jaws set in a deep frown, while Peter kept coming up to Jake's side, trying to whisper in his ear. Jake put up a hand to swat him away. He wanted to make up his own mind about the scene before hearing from Peter and Mack.

"What is this mumbo jumbo, Magrath?" McKenna demanded.

Jake stopped Edwin with a look. If he didn't, McKenna would get a longwinded, enthusiastic explanation for his latest contraption. Jake's assistant had been studying the work of a French policeman, Bertillon, who made a practice of taking photographs of crime scenes. Edwin had convinced Jake to buy a camera, and then he had engineered the contraption to allow him to position the camera directly above the dead body to take pictures. Prevented from voicing his explanation, Edwin flashed a bulb for a picture, causing McKenna to cover his eyes.

Furious, Chief McKenna walked over to Callahan and grabbed his shoulder. He slapped him in the face. "Take this man in," he told the uniformed man. "We'll get him to talk down at the station."

Jake shook his head. He couldn't control McKenna. He'd try to beat a confession out of Callahan. There was nothing Jake could do about that once the police had him at their station.

Peter stepped forward, and Jake clamped his mouth shut. The young detective had good intentions, but he hadn't learned yet that McKenna had the upper hand. "Mr. Callahan found the dead man, after he was beaten to death. He came in after Ian Stewart ran out, yelling that Lars was dead. It's Augustus Sumner who did it. Lars killed Conor Leary for him, and he was blackmailing Sumner, so Sumner killed him. He was here, drinking with Lars. Ian Stewart, the manager, can testify to that."

McKenna sizzled. "Right. You say Sumner, one of the most prominent businessmen in the city, beat this big Swede to death. So, where is he? Huh? Under the desk here? In that closet? Where is he? No. He's not here. But indicted murderer Callahan is here covered in blood. What do you call that? You're a fool is what you are, Attwood. Come on, men. Let's get back to the station and end this." He kicked one leg of the contraption that held the camera over the dead Lars, and Edwin rocked a bit on his stepladder. "If you think this hocus-pocus is going to prove something different, Magrath, you're crazy as these lunatics." He stomped out the door.

"But it was Sumner," Peter wailed to Jake. "He was here. We got his fingerprints on a glass for Edwin." He looked around. "Where's Ian Stewart?"

"Outside," Mack told him. "A bit sick, I think."

Lars certainly was a bloody mess. Jake could understand why the little Scottish man had to get some air. He listened as Peter poured out his story about Stewart bringing the fingerprints. He'd left Lars with Sumner and, when he returned, he found the bloody body and no sign of his employer. Peter hurried away to find the manager. Mack followed him.

Jake could see that Lars had been hit on the back of the head by an iron bar, probably from the discarded railway bridge on the Callahan property. It was the same method as the one used to kill Conor Leary. Jake let Edwin take multiple pictures, flash bulbs snapping and burning as he covered the room. In the cases of Ingrid and Leary, the bodies had been moved before the police arrived. Edwin hadn't been able to use his new toy. This scene was perfect, so Jake allowed him to take his time.

Peter returned with Ian Stewart. The manager corroborated Peter's story of how Sumner had welcomed Lars to the company with a drink. When Ian left to deliver the evidence to Peter, Sumner, and Lars were still in the office. When he returned, he found the dead man. He'd run away to get Peter, and when they arrived back at the scene, they found Callahan and Mack in the room. Ian looked worried.

Jake looked around for Mack to confirm what had happened. He called his name, and the big Irishman came in the doorway. "See what I found outside, in a barrel," he said. He held up a black overcoat stained with blood in the front. "A pair of gloves were stuffed in a pocket."

"That's Sumner's," Ian Stewart told them.

The orderlies from Massachusetts General Hospital had arrived to take the body away to the morgue. Mack handed Edwin the bloody overcoat.

Peter was beside himself. "It's Sumner. He did it, but McKenna won't even question him."

Mack raised an eyebrow. Jake and the ex-detective knew it would be difficult to get McKenna to consider anyone else now that he had a bloodstained Callahan in his clutches. He would have been smarting that his earlier arrest was countered by bail and the support of Honey Fitz and other local politicians who'd rallied behind Callahan. Peter didn't see it.

"We've got to go after Sumner," Peter said. "He could get away."

"Where would he go?" Jake asked. A wealthy man with the support of the Brahmin society and the local business community would not leave all his holdings behind.

Peter stared at him, and Ian Steward protested. "But Sumner was here with Lars. He must have killed him. Aren't you going to do anything?" His eyes blazed with anger.

Jake exchanged a glance with Mack. "We need proof," Jake said. "You can testify that you left Sumner with Lars, and when you returned, Lars was dead. But you did find Callahan with him."

Mack cleared his throat roughly. "I saw Stewart rush up the stairs at the house with a face like he'd seen a banshee. I ran over here when I heard him tell Attwood that Lars was dead. Bill was already here when I got through the door. He must have been trying to help poor Lars, but he was beyond help."

Ian Stewart collapsed onto a chair. Jake knew he was thinking about consequences for himself. If he testified against his employer, he'd have no job left. And if Sumner could escape suspicion, he wouldn't appreciate Ian's work with Peter behind his back. Jake felt sorry for him. "Give Edwin the glass with Sumner's prints," Jake told Peter. "We'll see if they match the rifle."

Peter realized he was still holding the bag, so he shoved it at Edwin. "Here. I'm going to find Sumner and talk to him. At the very least, he needs to say what he saw."

"McKenna won't thank you," Mack told him.

"McKenna be damned. I won't let Sumner get away with murder—again." Peter rushed out the door.

Jake nodded to Mack, who sighed and followed Peter. Jake hoped he could prevent the young detective from professional suicide, but he wouldn't bet on it.

Chapter Forty-Nine

Peter and Mack took the trolley through the tunnel and up to Beacon Hill, where Peter led the way to a townhouse on Chestnut Street. He was familiar with Sumner's address as he'd been to parties for the daughter's coming out the previous year. Like many wealthy Brahmins, Sumner had an estate north of Boston and a residence in the city.

Mack looked uncomfortable as Peter banged the lion's head knocker on the door.

A maid answered and led them to a study in the back of the house. Augustus Sumner sat in a well-padded leather armchair. He wore a velvet smoking jacket. He rose to his full height and cocked an eyebrow at the young detective. "Peter Attwood. How do you do? And who's this with you?"

Peter introduced Mack, and Sumner waved them to seats. "What can I do for you? Selling tickets to the policeman's ball, are you?" He smirked at them.

"No. This is serious. We need to ask you where you were this morning."

Sumner looked surprised. "Where I was? Here, of course. I haven't left the house today. Why?"

Peter felt the heat rising up his neck. He jumped up. "What do you mean, you've been here all day? You were in East Boston at the Sumner warehouse. You invited Lars Ericksson for a drink to celebrate hiring him for your company. And before you left, you beat Lars Ericksson to death with an iron bar."

Sumner stood up. "What are you talking about? How dare you come into my home and accuse me of such a thing? I have been here all morning. And what is this about Mr. Ericksson? You say he was killed?"

"Beaten to death in your office," Peter told him.

"I've heard nothing about this. I'll telephone Stewart." He pulled over a telephone on his desk.

"Stewart can swear you were there this morning. In fact, we have a whiskey glass with your fingerprints from when you were there. We can prove it."

"Nonsense. My staff can vouch for me being home all day. This is outrageous. How dare you accuse me?" Sumner was wild-eyed with rage. Peter hoped to provoke him further. He knew they didn't have proof of Sumner's guilt, and he wanted to make the man incriminate himself.

"You hired Conor Leary to sabotage Callahan's works so you could get the tunnel contract and when Leary tried to blackmail you, you got Ericksson to kill him. Or maybe you did it yourself like you killed Lars today."

"I've never heard such utter nonsense in my life. Get out of my house!" Sumner had grabbed the telephone, but he waved it in his hand like a weapon. "Get out! Or I'll call the police!"

"I am the police," Peter baited him. He stepped close enough to reach out for the telephone.

Mack stepped between the two men. "Now, now, let's not get excited."

Peter put up a hand to brush the big Irishman aside, but Mack swatted him back. "Let's get back to Dr. Magrath."

Peter was furious. "He can't get away with this just because he lives on Beacon Hill instead of East Boston."

Sumner moved toward the young detective, but Mack held him back. "Now, sir, let's just step back, shall we?" With one arm for each, he separated the men. "If you could just give us something that your fingers have touched, sir. We'll be going back to Dr. Magrath."

Sumner goggled at him.

"That's right, sir. A glass, say, or something like that." Mack picked up a wine glass from a display behind the desk. "This, sir. If you'd just grab it like."

Peter fumed. What was Mack doing? They already had a glass with Sumner's fingerprints. Peter almost found it comic that Mack had suddenly become an advocate for Edwin's scientific pursuits in criminal investigation. He expected Mack to be more in the beat-it-out-of-him camp like McKenna. But perhaps Mack, too, was intimidated by the status of someone like Sumner. It infuriated Peter.

Rolling his eyes, Sumner grasped the wine glass, then offered it to Mack. He seemed to want to show how much he spurned the accusations.

"If you have a little bag or something to put it in. We won't want to harm it, and we'll get it back to you, sir. But Dr. Magrath will want to examine it," Mack said. Peter saw that the reference to Jake was a magic word. Sumner knew of the medical examiner and was less likely to dismiss a request that seemed to come from him. After all, he was a Harvard man, too, Peter thought with disdain. Mack had succeeded in lowering the heat of passion in the room.

Bag in hand, Mack physically turned Peter around and pushed him toward the door. "Thank you for your assistance," he said as they departed.

Peter heard Sumner pick up the telephone and yell at the operator. Someone would pay for their intrusion. He hoped it wouldn't be his chief that Sumner was calling.

Chapter Fifty

Fanny was in the garage of the morgue when Peter and Mack returned. She had fashioned a few more props for the little replica of the three-decker house. Jake had told her that Lars was dead, and she felt sad as she looked at his meticulous work on the doll house.

Peter and Mack were arguing loudly, which brought Jake and Edwin out of the laboratory. Mack handed Edwin the bag. "From Mr. Sumner. He wants it back intact," Mack said.

Edwin held it gingerly, looking confused. "I already processed the other glass you brought. You were right. The fingerprints matched the ones on the barrel of the rifle that killed Mrs. Ericksson."

"See," Peter yelled. "I should have arrested Sumner! He did it. He framed Bill Callahan!"

"Stop," Jake demanded. "Explain." He sat on a stool. Fanny had already found a wooden chair near the miniature crime scene. Edwin slipped back into the laboratory. She knew he avoided conflict when he could. He found Mack and Peter too hot-blooded and noisy. Jake, on the other hand, wanted to hear their dispute.

"Look, this is what happened," Peter said. He stopped for a minute to look at the miniature. He looked around and grabbed a couple of shoe boxes. Emptying them of odds and ends, he placed them near the little three-decker. "Here's the Callahan works." He planted one upside-down box beside the house. "And here's Sumner's warehouse." He placed the other box longwise across from the first one. Then he took it up again and cut out a rectangle. "That's the window of Ian's office," he said.

185

Mack stepped up. Stooping forward, he grabbed some nails and dropped them by the Callahan works.

"Okay. That's the discarded railway bridge," Peter agreed. "Now, here's what happened." He looked in the top kitchen of the three-decker miniature and extracted a doll that represented Lars Ericksson. He placed him at the corner of the Callahan building. "Lars stood here and fired up at his wife."

Fanny took a tiny rifle from her satchel and handed it to Peter. She had found some guns in the arms of toy soldiers in a shop on Charles Street. They were just what she needed.

"Right." He put it beside the Lars doll. "So, he shoots his wife, but he hides the rifle maybe in the storage box. Then Ian comes to his window." Peter pointed. "And sees him."

"But Lars was in his kitchen," Mack pointed out.

"Well, he must have hurried up the steps and back to his apartment." Peter walked the doll past the face-down doll that was Ingrid and up the stairs.

Mack pointed at the doll on the second-floor porch. "Kate was on the porch. She would have seen him."

"Maybe he hid from her."

"Nobody can hide from Kate," Mack grumbled.

"Who else was there?" Jake asked.

"I came out, and Leary was there, and Ian," Mack said.

"I'm not sure Lars could have gotten back to the kitchen without being seen," Fanny said.

Peter explained his theory that Sumner had given Lars the rifle, and then Sumner had gotten Lars to kill Leary in exchange for keeping quiet.

"You're starting from an assumption that Sumner is responsible," Jake said. "You need to approach the scene without previous assumptions."

"But it fits," Peter said. "Why else would anyone kill Ingrid? Unless you believe Callahan killed her to cover up a romantic entanglement."

Mack was weary. "I told you. Ingrid was with me; there was no other man. But Lars was jealous. He's the only one vicious enough to kill her."

Mack was still mourning his lover and feeling guilty about her death. He was too sure of his assumption that Lars had killed her, just as Peter wanted to believe Sumner was behind it all. Fanny noticed Peter fingering one of the full-size real rifles that were lying on the broad table. "Be careful," she reminded him. "Remember the ricochets that happened when one of those rifles was fired the first time."

He stepped back from the table as if burned. "Right. Ricochet." He stared into space.

Edwin came in from the laboratory, holding a glass in his hand. "Peter, did you say you got this glass from Mr. Sumner? Are you sure these are his fingerprints?"

Peter didn't seem to hear. Mack responded. "Yes. I got him to hold the glass in front of my eyes. Those are his prints."

"Then whose are those on the other glass?" Edwin held up the tumbler from the Sumner warehouse. "The prints on this first glass match the ones on the rifle. But the ones from the new glass are different, completely different."

Chapter Fifty-One

Mack drove the rickety Suffolk Sue while Peter held onto his seat with both hands. They jumped to the front of the ferry line using Peter's badge. Mack clutched the steering wheel. Peter didn't dare get out of the motor for fear of being left behind. The ferry bumped over some waves as Peter hunched against the wind.

On shore, they barreled through the streets of East Boston with Magrath's sirens blaring. When Peter had explained his theory back at the morgue, Mack's eyes lit up with enthusiasm. A telephone call to Sumner's home reached a manservant. His master had gone to his warehouse to question Ian Stewart. Fearing a confrontation between the two men, Peter had called the East Boston station to tell them to go to the Sumner warehouse. He insisted they stop Sumner. Jake allowed Peter to pursue Sumner in his Model T with the provision that Mack go with him.

As they lurched into the yard between the Callahan and Sumner buildings, Peter jumped down.

"No one here, sir," a uniformed officer told him from the doorway of Sumner's warehouse. He and several other officers came out the door, looking puzzled. "I thought you said there was a possible incident."

A muffled shot rang out. It was from the Callahan building.

The men stiffened and then rushed over. Peter beat them to the door, where he spread his arms to hold them back. "Wait here. Let me check."

Mack pushed his way through the men. "What're you doing?" The medical examiner had told Mack to keep the inexperienced detective from danger. But Peter was tired of inexperience as an excuse for his mistakes. He thought he'd already made a major error, and if he didn't handle it, a man could die. There'd already been a gunshot. Peter didn't know what he'd find inside, but if Mack rushed in, followed by uniformed men, there could be a bloodbath. "Stay back, I've got this," he told Mack, who growled at him.

Peter entered the building, closing the door behind him. "Ian Stewart," he called. "It's Detective Attwood. Are you all right?"

He heard a scuffle and a groan from his right. He followed a corridor to an open door into a wide room full of building supplies. Piles of boxes, drums of oil, stacks of huge wooden pilings stood around the room. Peter leaned around some boxes to see. "Are you there?"

At the far end of the room, Ian Stewart stood with a pistol pointed at a lump of clothes on the ground. That must be Sumner. The prone man moved, rising to his hands and knees. Blood dripped from a wound on Augustus Sumner's scalp. He moaned and collapsed onto his back.

"Stay down," Ian ordered. He looked across at Peter. "Thank God you got here. He was going to kill me. He pulled out the gun and forced me over here. He rigged the place with dynamite. But I got the gun away."

Peter felt a chill down his spine. In the light from a lantern balanced on a pile of boxes, he could see sticks of dynamite bound together and pushed into a stack of crates. A long fuse was draped across and hung down behind Ian. Peter had never used the stuff, but he knew it was dangerous. He needed to worry about the gun first. He swallowed.

"Good work, Ian. Put down the gun, and we'll take him in," Peter said. He hid his own gun behind his back. The little Scottish man looked nervous. His hand shook with terror. He pointed the gun at Sumner on the ground.

"He's moving!" Ian shouted. With both hands on the gun, he cocked it.

"Stop," Peter yelled, pulling his own pistol out and aiming it at Ian. "Stop, Ian. I know it was you."

Glassy-eyed, Ian looked across at him. "It's Sumner. He tried to kill me."

"No, it was you. I know, Ian. You hired Conor Leary to cause those accidents at the Callahan work sites. Then you killed him when he demanded more money." Ian blinked, and Peter tried to distract him. "Why did you do that?" Peter asked. He honestly couldn't understand what had driven the

189

little manager to such drastic actions. He waited.

"Him." Ian's hands dipped as he used the pistol to point at his employer. "Ever since that accident that killed three men, we've been losing contracts to Callahan. He blamed me." Ian glared at Sumner, who was barely conscious on the floor. "That dirty Irish Mick. Him with his certificates and his political pals." Ian looked vicious as he squeezed his face in revulsion. Peter realized Ian hated that the social climbing Bill Callahan had managed to pull himself up above Ian in the social scale.

Peter glanced around. He was twenty feet away from Ian, whose gun was still cocked. He saw a pile of wooden two-by-fours near the wall on his right. His path to Ian was blocked by heavy barrels, and he wasn't sure of his aim. If he missed, Ian would kill Sumner. Peter slid forward a few feet.

"Stay where you are!" Ian yelled, moving the gun to point at the detective, who could tell he was adjusting to the idea the Peter knew the truth. Ian glared down at Sumner again, the cause of all his misery.

"Callahan? You blamed Callahan?" Peter kept him talking, hoping to distract him from his intent to shoot the man on the floor or Peter himself.

"Why should he get so far ahead?" Ian demanded, taking his gaze off Sumner long enough to glance across at Peter. His naked anger startled Peter.

Ian turned back to point the gun at Sumner. "At least Callahan worked at getting the contracts. This lazy bastard stuck his pointed nose in the air and expected to win just because of his filthy name. His father wouldn't have let these dirty Irish immigrants take away business. He knew how to keep them down where they belonged."

Ian Stewart was also an immigrant, but Peter realized now wasn't the time to mention that fact. He hadn't realized how deeply the Scottish man resented Callahan's success.

"So, you hired Leary to make trouble for Callahan?"

"That drunk, Leary, would do anything for money." He grinned across at Peter, and the young detective felt a chill reach across from the little man. "He didn't like that Bill was getting above himself, either. He liked a wee dram, did Conor Leary, and it loosened his mouth, so he told how he was not appreciated. We sympathized. So, when I offered him a bit of money to make a little trouble, he agreed easily."

Peter realized that Ian had cold-bloodedly recruited Conor Leary by playing on the man's weakest points. He got him drunk and reveled in his resentments. "But Leary changed his mind then?" Peter slid another foot forward. The closer he was, the more likely he was to hit the target. Ideally, he could wrestle the gun from the angry little man.

"Hah. That drunk wanted more money. He said he'd tell Mr. Sumner here." Ian waggled the gun at his employer, who looked up in horror at the barrel. "Stay still," Ian demanded. He smiled a little when Sumner stiffened in fear.

There was a noise at the back of the room, behind the pile of crates where Ian was standing.

"What's that?" Ian yelled. "Don't come in here. If there's any funny business, this whole place will go up." He pointed his gun at the packet of dynamite. "I'll light this, and we'll all go up."

"Stop. No. No one is coming. I told them to wait," Peter yelled. "Don't do it, Ian." He could see Ian hunch in preparation. Ian took one hand off the gun and rummaged in a pocket. Peter raked his mind for something to distract him. "You killed Ingrid Ericksson by mistake, didn't you?"

That hit a nerve. "You figured that out?"

"You took Sumner's rifle and aimed at Leary, but he was near the storage bin and your shot ricocheted against the iron of the discarded railroad bridge and hit Ingrid on the porch. She fell down dead."

Ian actually laughed. "I didn't know it. Nobody did. We just heard Kate Gallagher yell, and everyone went to look. I didn't know it was the shot that killed her till you came asking questions."

And that was the start of it all. "So, you decided to frame Bill Callahan for the death."

Ian smiled. "It was easy to get Lars to think Ingrid was seeing Callahan." Ian pulled out a lighter and held it in his right hand while his left still pointed the gun at Sumner, groaning on the floor.

"You took a handkerchief from Kate's basket," Peter said. Was Ian crazy enough to really light the fuse? Surely, he knew he'd be blown to hell with Sumner. And so would Peter.

"With his initials embroidered on it. Would you believe it? A shanty Irish like him with his initials on the linen. It was a farce."

"But Lars believed it." Peter slid another step closer. How to tackle the man before he ignited the fuse?

"I knew Sumner here was trying to lure Lars away from Callahan. He even had me approach that stupid Swede with a job offer. After all my years and all my loyalty. His father would never have treated me like that. Choosing a dumb Swede who could barely speak English over me."

"You wanted to get Lars to kill Bill Callahan for you," Peter said. He realized that was why Ian had planted the dynamite in Callahan's warehouse and forced Sumner to go there. He wanted to destroy both men.

"But that stupid Swede was too dumb to do anything about it. He just whined about Callahan and his wife. What kind of man is that?"

"So, you took the rifle and planted it in Bill's car at the yacht club in Marblehead." Peter wanted to know everything, even if he was blown to bits. He was not at all sure he could reach Ian before the madman blew them all up.

Ian kicked the man at his feet. "This lump of shit was handing over his boat to those Micks and going into business with them. Fool that he is."

"You told the Gustin gang about their plans." Peter suddenly realized this fact. Ian grinned. "You'd taken care of Leary already."

"Leary thought he was getting more money, but he got a pipe to the head instead." Ian had a mad grin on his face.

"The same way you killed Lars."

Ian's face reddened, and he stamped a foot. He raised the lighter and flicked it on. "After all that, this slithering snake told me to hire the dumb Swede. After all that."

"No," Peter yelled, rushing forward.

Ian aimed at Sumner but was hit with a two-by-four before he could pull the trigger.

Ian dropped to the ground like a puppet whose strings were cut. Mack grabbed the gun and kicked the lighter out of Ian's hand.

Peter stared at the big Irishman, feeling his blood drain to his feet. "I told you to wait outside," he whispered.

"Well, you didn't really expect me to do that, did you?"

Chapter Fifty-Two

When Fanny arrived at the Grove Street Morgue the next day, she met Peter at the door. "You had an exciting day yesterday," she said. "How did McKenna react when you brought in the real killer?"

"Flummoxed," Peter said. "Not much he could do about it. He had to let Callahan go, especially since Sumner was there singing my praises."

"Good for you."

Peter frowned. "I tried to get McKenna to reinstate Mack, but he wasn't having any of it. Mack saved the day, but it doesn't matter to the higher-ups in the department. They'll never hire him back. I feel really bad about that."

Edwin answered the bell and let them in. They found Jake and Mack in the garage. The big Irishman was trying to fit the miniature of the three-decker house into a packing box. Fanny was surprised to see Mack had a big grin on his face. She hoped he wasn't counting on Peter having gotten his job back for him. She found a chair and steeled herself for an explosion when the Irishman heard the worst.

Peter looked worried, but Mack ordered him to help lift the house. With a few swear words, they managed to lower the miniature into the crate that Edwin held in place for them.

Mack clapped his hands together, wiping off the sawdust from the little house. "Good. I promised Kate I'd bring it back for poor little Lilly."

"She's lost both her parents now, hasn't she? How awful," Fanny said.

"Aye, but Kate's happy as a clam to finally have a wee girlie," Mack said. "I brought a wagon to get this back to her. She's too little to know what's going on, but Kate'll spoil her to death. She's so happy to have another female in the family."

Fanny remembered that Kate had seven brothers and three sons. She could sympathize with her excitement to have a daughter. "She'll be able to keep her?"

Jake spoke up from where he was seated on a stool at the workbench. "It's the best plan for the poor child."

"Dr. Magrath helped with the authorities." Mack smiled broadly.

Peter cleared his throat. "Mack, I want to thank you for your help yesterday. Ian Stewart was going to blow the place up."

Mack grinned, and Peter took a big breath. "I'm sorry your help isn't appreciated by my superiors. I tried to get them to give you back your job, but I wasn't successful. I'm sorry."

Mack's grin got wider. Jake stood up. "Well, I'm glad to say that won't be necessary," he said, turning to Mack. "I've hired the ex-detective to be an investigator for the medical examiner. He starts tomorrow."

Peter's mouth dropped open.

Mack stepped over and clapped him on the back. "You've not seen the last of me yet, my boy!"

Jake smiled. He looked at Fanny. "With Edwin busy at his classes and more involved with the laboratory work, I convinced the authorities I needed help."

Fanny nodded. She was sure Jake could get whatever he needed from the authorities. He was both respected and needed.

Jake cocked his head at her as Peter congratulated Mack, shaking his hand. "I'll still need you for taking notes," he reassured Fanny. "And perhaps we can get at least one homicide detective to go about it the right way."

Jake was unusually optimistic. They would still need to deal with McKenna and his ilk. She doubted the chief detective would welcome any help from Magrath and especially Mack. And the new scientific methods Edwin was so interested in still needed to be tested in court. Certainly, the deep rift this case had revealed between Fanny's Brahmin friends on Beacon Hill and the new immigrants, especially the Irish, was unlikely to shrink. The rumblings of hatred beneath the surface of polite society were like tremors preceding an earthquake. But, for now, the Callahans and the Sumners could resume their competitions as if the angry Ian Stewart had never struck out at them. He'd confessed to his crimes and would be sent to prison.

She smiled. She was glad she'd been able to participate in the investigation and contribute to it. Jake didn't need to find money to pay her. He wouldn't need to get approval to call on her for help. That satisfied her—for now. But she thought there was a lot more they could do to improve methods of investigation, just as they had discussed. And she was in a good position to prod that movement along. "Legal Medicine" was what Jake called it. Fanny would work to get it recognized as a legitimate field of study. She felt she'd found her crusade and was determined to gear up to fight for it.

Epilogue

September 1953

Private dining room of the Ritz Carlton Hotel, Boston

Fanny sat at the head of the table and was satisfied that her men were getting the proper treatment. Waiters delivered plates of tenderloin steaks and kept wine and liquor glasses filled. The group had spent a busy week listening to scientists and police investigators and participating in classes that required them to demonstrate their own techniques. They deserved the fancy dinner as a reward.

She turned to the man at her right. "Captain Wilson, thank you for agreeing to demonstrate interrogation methods this year. I've heard a lot of praise for your sessions."

"My pleasure. Call me Frank, Captain Lee." He grinned. He was in his fifties, balding, with a wide smile. Captain of the homicide division of the Boston Police Department, Fanny knew the FBI had recently solicited his help with the Brinks robbery case. He was respected by prosecutors and defense attorneys. He was also the highest-ranking Negro officer in the city.

"I fear my rank is more honorary than yours," Fanny told him. The New Hampshire State Police had conferred the title as thanks for her help over the years. Wilson was canny to compliment her on her one vanity. It tickled her to be addressed as "Captain Lee." Her relentless advocacy for better training of police and the move to replace the political coroner system with medical examiners entitled her to the honor, though. She was proud of her accomplishments and thought her old friend Jake Magrath would have been proud of her, too. He had died just before she began her countrywide crusade to replace coroners with medical examiners.

On her left, the head of the Massachusetts State Police finished his steak with a sigh. "Delicious. Thanks so much for inviting me again, Mrs….ah, Captain Lee." For several years, the Harvard Homicide Seminars had been held twice a year, and Fanny hosted the special dinner at the conclusion of the week. She knew police officials around New England, and more recently the whole country, vied for an invitation. Wiping his mouth with the linen napkin, the man pointed to Wilson. "I'll bet you didn't know our premier homicide detective here has something in common with you. Believe it or not, he's reputed to be handy with a needle and thread. They say that after a big case winds up, Mrs. Wilson gets a new set of drapes!"

Wilson chuckled. "That's true. I have to say I admire the needlework in your miniatures," he said.

Fanny was a bit surprised. "How ever did you learn to sew?" she asked.

"Well, it's not all by hand, you know. I have a machine. My daughter's a figure skater. She needed costumes while she was growing up, and they're awfully expensive. That's what got me started."

Fanny knew that Wilson came from a distinguished family in Roxbury. His father had been a prominent attorney, and his siblings had graduated from Harvard and Radcliffe. Wilson had enlisted in the army during WWI and became a policeman afterward. But mastery of a sewing machine was not something she would have expected.

He saw her confusion. "It's actually relaxing, don't you think?" he asked with a twinkle in his eye. She knew he dealt with bloody crimes and nasty hoodlums. It was hard to picture him bent over drapes. But she felt a sudden connection to him. "Yes," he nodded. "After dealing with tragedies, sitting down to make something with your own hands can be satisfying, don't you think? And, of course, it demands all your attention to get it right. Do you know what I'm talking about?"

She did. Fanny remembered the obsession that had taken over her days at the end of the war when she had created the miniature crime scenes that were used in the homicide seminars. They were fictional death scenes but based on composites of scenes she had visited and discussed with Jake Magrath before his death in 1938. It was a dark time for her after Jake's death and the deaths of her daughter, her parents, and her brother. And the terrible war, of course. She had become obsessed with the idea of reproducing some of the cases she remembered from working with Jake. She had spent day and night up in her New Hampshire home creating the tiny scenes of death. The detailed work blocked out everything else while she created the miniatures. It drained the excess energy that had built up. Completion of each scene brought relief. She looked into the eyes of Captain Wilson and realized he had shared that kind of experience.

She smiled in acknowledgment. "I heard that you participated in the exercise using the nutshell studies," she said. Wilson had been asked to demonstrate interrogation techniques to the students, but he had asked to do one of the nutshell studies. The miniature crime scenes were kept in a special room in the Harvard Legal Medicine department. Students of the seminar were given background information about the scene, witness statements, etc. Then, they were tasked with reporting their observations. "I understand that you're the first person assigned the Two-Story Porch nutshell who suggested the death might have resulted from a stray bullet. That was very perceptive of you."

"Ah, yes. I suppose it takes some experience to realize that sometimes the explanation can depend on a random action. A shooting is usually done with intention, but nobody would try to shoot a woman above them on a porch. It wouldn't work."

"So, the result was unintentional," Fanny agreed. The scenario for the case study had a solution that several boys had been playing with a gun, and a shot had gone astray and killed the woman hanging clothes on the second-floor porch.

But Fanny suddenly remembered the three-decker in East Boston where Ingrid Ericksson had died. The bullet intended for Conor Leary had ricocheted off the broken pieces of the train bridge and struck the young mother. Faces from the past, Lars, Mack, Peter, and Kate floated up from Fanny's memory. And Jake. That had been the beginning of Jake's tutoring investigators, a task she had shouldered after his death. Looking down the long table at the men from this week's seminar, she knew Jake would approve.

"Good work, Frank," she told Captain Wilson. "And now, I think it's time for our toast to my old friend." She stood up, and the men went quiet. "To Dr. George Burgess Magrath," Fanny said, raising her glass. "May he approve of all your work this week, and may that help you all in your efforts to convict the guilty, clear the innocent, and find the truth in a nutshell."

Afterword

I have purposely set the stories in the Nutshell Murder Mystery series in the 1920s. Although Frances Glessner Lee actually created the nutshell studies of unexplained death in the 1940s, I want to explore how she became so interested in criminal investigation. The tiny scenes that were used to train police investigators were not based on specific crimes. And they do not have solutions as such. They are composites of actual crimes.

In this series, I imagine Mrs. Lee encountering real crime scenes with her longtime friend Dr. Magrath. She is also learning about the state of the science of investigation, which was expanding at the time. She meets the men who are investigators. In the first book she's drawn in because one of the young men in her home for returning soldiers is accused. In the second book, she has been bitten by a growing infatuation with the work of criminal investigation to "convict the guilty, clear the innocent, and find the truth in a nutshell." The stories in the series will describe some fictional cases that involve her so deeply that when she inherits her fortune in the 1930s she invests money in Harvard's department of Legal Medicine. After Dr. Magrath's death in 1938, she creates her set of miniature crime scenes to be used to train investigators. I hope that explains the choice to set the stories in the 1920s.

I chose East Boston because I knew little about it, but I realized that both my father and my mother's families lived there in the early 1920s. So, the McNally and Callahan families are very roughly based on the McNamaras and Ellises. Like Kate Gallagher, my grandmother had seven brothers and six sons. She had to be a tough lady to manage them all. Her husband was a soft-spoken Boston fireman who was later invalided out. Later in the decade, the family moved to Clinton, Massachusetts where more relatives from County Mayo had settled. I've heard that my grandmother said she had to move her sons out of East Boston before they got arrested for fighting with Italians who were moving in.

William H. Ellis and Son was a family company that built many docks and wharves in Boston and the Massachusetts shore. Like Old Will in the story, my great-grandfather was a ships' carpenter working for McKay, the famous yacht designer. He started his own business later and brought his son, my grandfather, into it while his other son, Herbert, had a career in the Navy. They lived in the house on Meridian Street in the 1920s, although the works they could see out the back windows in the story are fictional. Like Joe Kennedy, my grandfather later moved out of East Boston to Brookline.

My filmmaker cousin, Maureen McNamara, took me on a tour of East Boston to the street where the McNamaras lived, and we found the house where the Ellises lived. I had to change and move them closer together for my story. The characters are only very roughly based on my ancestors. But it was fun thinking about what it was like to live at that time, when my grandparents were young. My father was born in 1920 and my mother in 1921, so they weren't on the scene yet.

Augustus Sumner is a complete fabrication. He's not based on any real person and the competition with the Callahan company is all made up. The deep division between the Irish and the Brahmins in Boston was real and remnants of it were still obvious when I was young. It was a big deal that the Kennedy's were not allowed to join "The Country Club" in Brookline because they were Catholic and an even bigger deal when JFK became president. James Michael Curley was still a memorable character at the time. John Francis "Honey Fitz" Fitzgerald was a very real person, serving as Boston's mayor and as a member of the US House of Representatives. He would later be famous as the maternal grandfather of John F. Kennedy, Robert Kennedy, and Teddy Kennedy.

I remember my father got a big kick out of it when he dined at the Wellesley College Club. My first job was in the library there and I joined their lovely club as staff. "Old Yankee" prejudices against the Irish were still very real when my parents were young. Like Fanny, I found that this division was a feature of Boston that I didn't see in Chicago. Not that there weren't plenty of ethnic groups in Chicago vying for power. I've described some of that in my Emily Cabot Mysteries. But the longstanding feuds between the Old Yankees and Irish seem to be peculiar to Boston.

The Gustin Gang were real. They got involved in the illegal liquor trade during Prohibition. They were in South Boston while the Italians were in the North End. They both used rum runners, boats that sailed out beyond the international border to pick up booze and smuggle it in.

The problem of how to reach East Boston from the city center was a real issue. The scene where Eileen Callahan describes a proposed tunnel project is from newspaper accounts at the time and the resulting postponement of the tunnel in favor of more ferry boats was the result in 1920. The Sumner Tunnel wasn't opened until 1934 and it carried two-way traffic until the Callahan Tunnel was built in 1961. (I have borrowed those two surnames for my fictional characters.) The Ted Williams Tunnel opened in 1995 and was part of the "Big Dig." The original tunnel, for the subway only was built in 1904 and is still in use.

Boston's "Inner Harbor" is what separates it from East Boston and Charlestown. So near and yet so far. Logan Airport in East Boston was largely constructed on landfill. It's difficult to picture Boston without a map. I find the map for the harbor water taxis the most useful. I have also sailed out of Courageous Sailing in Charlestown. You get a better idea of the shape of the city from the water.

Thanks to my cousin Deane Illk, out in Minnesota, who loaned me a diary of my grandmother (the prototype for Eileen Callahan) and some other information. Also, thanks to Tom McNamara, another cousin, who shared some of the family history he has collected about East Boston. And, of course, thanks to Maureen McNamara who is also a collector of family stories.

Boston Police Captain Frank Wilson was a real person who was appointed Superintendent before his death. He was famous as the head of homicide for many years. When my father was Boston Police Commissioner in the tumultuous 1960s, I remember him ruing the fact that an African American head of homicide, who had been his mentor during the Brinks robbery case when he was an FBI agent, had died before his appointment as Commissioner. He would have liked to have his mentor by his side. I was reminded of this when the first African American officer was made Boston Police Commissioner, so I fantasized that Frank Wilson might lecture at one of Mrs. Lee's Harvard Homicide Seminars. She died around the time my father was appointed in 1962 and I never got to ask him if he'd known her before his death in 2000.

At the time of the story, various forensic techniques were in development. Some of the sources for information on fingerprinting, ballistics and crime photography include *The Killer of Little Shepherds: A True Crime Story and the Birth of Forensic Science by* Douglas Starr; *Silent Witnesses: The Often Gruesome but Always Fascinating History of Forensic Science* by Nigel McCrery; *Forensics: What Bugs, Burns, Prints, DNA, and More Tell Us About Crime* by Val McDermid.

For more information on the Boston Police Strike, see *A City in Terror: 1919, the Boston police strike* by Francis Russell.

The *Nutshell Studies of Unexplained Death* offer many more crime scenes to make into stories. And there's plenty of history in Boston to explore. I hope you'll watch for more books in the Nutshell Murder Mystery series. I'm planning on researching Boston's West End for the next book. That neighborhood is famous for having disappeared in the urban renewal projects of the 1960s. But it is still remembered and celebrated. Thanks for reading the series. Please contact me through my website francesmcnama.com if you have questions or suggestions.

Acknowledgements

Thanks to my writing group, Leslie Wheeler, Katherine Fast, Cheryl Marceau, and Mark Ammons. Also, to my former editor and current reader, Emily Victorson. Thanks to the staff of Level Best Books. Any errors are all my own.

About the Author

Frances McNamara grew up in Boston, where her father served as Police Commissioner for ten years. She has degrees from Mount Holyoke and Simmons Colleges and retired from the University of Chicago. She now divides her time between Boston and Cape Cod.

She is the author of the Emily Cabot Mystery series in addition to the Nutshell Murders series.

SOCIAL MEDIA HANDLES:

https://www.facebook.com/francesmcnamaraAuthor/

https://twitter.com/FMcNamaraAuthor

https://www.linkedin.com/in/frances-mcnamara-271257123/

https://www.instagram.com/francesmcnamaraauthor/

https://www.pinterest.com/fdmcnama/_saved/

https://www.goodreads.com/author/show/2728513.Frances_McNamara?from_search=true

https://www.bookbub.com/authors/frances-mcnamara

https://www.amazon.com/Frances-McNamara/e/B002BO9QK8/ref=sr_ntt_srch_lnk_1?qid=1523634851&sr=1-1

https://www.youtube.com/channel/UCZh33-BofivPN-2o6ep_k0w

AUTHOR WEBSITE:
https://francesmcnamara.com/

Also by Frances McNamara

Nutshell Murder Mystery series
Molasses Murder in a Nutshell

Emily Cabot Mysteries
Death at the Fair
Death at Hull House
Death at Pullman
Death at Woods Hole
Death at Chinatown
Death at the Paris Exposition
Death at Selig Studios
Death on the Homefront
Death in a Time of Spanish Flu

Printed in the USA
CPSIA information can be obtained
at www.ICGtesting.com
JSHW022035100224
56975JS00005B/200